CW01500899

Justin Robertson is a renowned DJ, author, music producer, visual artist and broadcaster. For the past 30 years, he has been a leading figure in the dance music world, falling in love with electronic music whilst completing a degree in philosophy at The University of Manchester. He headlines clubs and festivals around the globe as a DJ and formerly with his band Lionrock.

As well as his own musical productions, he is much in demand as a remixer, having worked with the likes of Bjork, New Order, Noel Gallagher & Erasure over the years. In the past decade, he has exhibited six acclaimed collections of his art around the UK and Europe, including producing a soundtrack and book to accompany them. He hosts two popular shows, The Temple of Wonders and The Rotating Institute, bimonthly on Soho Radio.

He has written for Ransom Note, The Social and The Guardian on music, travel and philosophical matters, interviewing the likes of Rob Newman and Gary Lachman. His debut novel, The Tangle, was published in 2021 and is currently being adapted for television.

First published by Velocity Press 2025

velocitypress.uk

Copyright © Justin Robertson 2025

Printed and bound in Great Britain by Clays Ltd, Elcograf S.p.A.

Cover design
Hayden Russell

Cover image
Justin Robertson

Typesetting
Paul Baillie-Lane
www.ingenious-books.com

Justin Robertson has asserted his right under the Copyright, Designs and Patents Act 1988 to be identified as the author of this work

All rights reserved. No part of this publication may be reproduced, in any form or by any means, without permission from the publisher

ISBN: 9781913231804

the trial of jonah

justin robertson

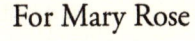
For Mary Rose

1

all rise

An old, bent and crooked judge wearing a wig that has seen more crime than care walks into a court room. A crusty relic from an ancient tradition of jurisprudence. He is here to pass judgement on a miserable sinner. The court is packed with the victims' angry relatives. The press pack snap and scribble. A gaggle of freakily attired sympathisers blow kisses at the accused. In the dock a small boy of maybe eight years old grins and waves back at them. He is wearing an exquisite suit cut in the style of a 'Young Americans' era David Bowie. It is clearly too big for the small boy, though once it may have fitted him perfectly. A cry of 'all rise' cuts above the clamour. The murmurs in the court subside as everyone gets to their feet. A gavel descends. Clonk! The court is now in session.

✗

Panning shot of a bright blue planet Earth: small islands of land are visible through beautiful billowing cloud formations. The camera pulls back to reveal an elegant spacecraft approaching the planet. The craft hums with a melodious tone that sounds like controlled guitar feedback. The camera retreats through the windshield of the spacecraft to reveal a complex control panel covered with a variety of flashing readouts and elaborate dials. At the centre of the panel is a steering wheel, much like the ones found in vintage sports cars. The camera focuses on two graceful hands gripping the wheel. The pilot is whistling a tune.

Where should stories start? At the beginning? That seems like a ridiculous place to begin. Nothing interesting ever happens at the beginning. The beginning of life? When is that? When does life start? Conception, birth, the first moment of self-realisation, first concept formed, first fuck, first dip in the baptismal pool, first draw on the chalice? No, the beginning seems like a wholly inadequate place to start a story. Infants may possess a certain purity of thought, but they are terrible raconteurs. And in any case, once the world becomes word it loses that essential essence of emptiness that children instinctively feel.

Why? That is the first question. You may believe your baby's first word was 'mamma' or 'papa', but that was only their first word in a language you could understand. For months your child has been screaming out, 'Why!?' Because children are born from the emptiness to which all things return. They are time travellers returned from their own future. Screaming out. Why!? So don't ask them to tell you a decent story, they are still too annoyed about being born to be worrying about narrative arcs. Nor can we rely on later adult recollections. Though we long for the clarity of that suckling wisdom, it is impossible to recapture. Memories are too insubstantial and unformed; everything is guesswork tainted by hindsight and wishful thinking. No, the beginning seems a most unsatisfactory place to start. The end is where stories begin.

My name, as far as I can recall, is Jonah Plantagenet. Household name. Renowned record producer, remixer and performer, the most successful disc jockey that has ever existed, feted artist and celebrated author. And I am dead. Being dead is great. I love it. I didn't think I'd take to it at first, but it really is the most fun I've ever had. And to think we spend all our lives worrying about it. In fact, the whole shaky edifice of human civilisation is one great extended ritual designed to cope with the prospect of non-existence. Being dead is very relaxing, much more relaxing than dying, which was a pain in the arse. In my case, dying involved a long, convoluted ceremony that lasted several days, which was not only cripplingly expensive but also extremely uncomfortable. The soaring price of a knife sharpener's services. Cold paving and stone altar. Terrible drafts, hellish gusts. But once the ritual was completed and the sacrificial scythe had slashed its last grim incision, it really was plain sailing. All that trying to make sense of life stuff had been a waste of time. Sense was the problem. Being senseless was the tricky part. Life was fun, for sure, and diverting, certainly. Diverting? Yeah, that's what I was doing, diverting. Avoiding living by worrying about being alive when I should have just got on with it. I mean I nearly got there, eventually, with all that painting, scribbling, writing and all that fucking music! Yes, that was pretty close. In the sweat pit, mosh dance, paint-daubed basements, as the kick drum mantra dissolved the barriers. That was close. In the brush strokes of Turner or Hilma af Klint's divine diagrams, the incantations of Ballard, Catling and Burroughs, anywhere the veil was thin enough to get a glimpse of the greater beauty. That was fucking close. But here in the void, here in nothing, that's where it's at. 'I' is 'we' are 'you' are 'me' and 'we' are all together. In no-thing. In no-when.

Before death we were all living inside a spell. The miraculous was manifest in every breath, in every step and every thought. We have forgotten this simple truth because we never really knew it. Any wisdom we ever had was slowly dissolved by age. Time eventually erodes any vestiges of wonder and mocks the thoughts of children as being mere fantasies born of ignorance, when they are in reality the only thoughts we ever have that are in any way true. The judge will no doubt rule all my childhood insights as inadmissible in the court of public opinion, by reason of insanity. But the little I can recall of my earliest years are the only true words I will utter, in this, my criminal trial. Everything else, every memory and statement, will have been fed through the filter of millions of years of human skulduggery and should be discounted. Only as a child did I see the spell uncoiling in the shadows of my local wood or in the fabric of my home.

I have no idea how you will have come across this book. It may be on a shelf with a sign. Classic authors A-Z. You found it under P, for Plantagenet. Or perhaps you found it in a charity shop store room amongst a pile of other unwanted copies. In a landfill site. In an evidence locker. Perhaps you snuck a peak under the bedsheets after lights out and before the purity police came knocking. Perhaps you saved it from the bonfire. You might be reading this after seeing me on television, presuming you still have such things, or as a meme, or as a multi-episodic podcast. Or maybe you saw my name on a list of forbidden thinkers, sinners, apostates. A list of fiends. You may be asking yourself what makes him tick. How did he come to do such monstrous things? Maybe you're hoping to find out by reading this book. On discovery, I suspect this manuscript will be seized by the authorities. Offered in evidence perhaps. At the very least examined for clues; clues as to why I took such diabolical liberties with the souls I fed off. I can assure you none of them suffered unduly. Most survived intact or only slightly disfigured. It was necessary, as you will soon appreciate. Such is the way with confessions; they are usually prolonged pleas for understanding and forgiveness. This is not. The point I'm trying to make is: I'm not sorry. I am nothing. Now don't for one moment think this gives any of you a free pass to do what thou wilt. It didn't work for Crowley, and it won't work for you either. See, I've done terrible things. Cruel things. But I've done my time. Quite literally, as it happens, because I am, or should I say was, or even will be, a time traveller. That was the price I had to pay. To live is to suffer. Endless rotations on the wheel. A million lifetimes and a million faces. A gift and a curse. Endless heartache. Parking tickets. Plague. Flood. Famine. Queues at festivals for warm lager. Hatchbacks with faulty rubber seals. War. Badly fitting loafers. Poor stitching. Meteor collisions. Vending machine sandwiches. The eternal rebirth into different bodies at different times with different haircuts and different clothes and different tastes. But always humanity. Confused. Lost. Looking for life. But suffering isn't all bad; for one, it gives you a certain sense of perspective. Actually – and don't tell God this – but living really was a gas at times, proper living that is, you know the one where the fog lifts? The one where the dew hangs on the spider's web, where the sunlight refracting through the tiny droplets that hang on its gossamer threads is transformed into a beautiful rainbow? The one where Ken Booth is singing on the stereo? That kind of life. And you should never apologise for that.

2

the arrival of rock and roll

The old judge peers over his half-moon spectacles and demands that the defence council explain themselves. He wants to know why they have entered such a clearly fabricated piece of evidence into the official trial record.

Son of a Demon God. That's what it says on the poorly photocopied title page. It looks like a sixth former's first attempt at a fanzine rather than a thoroughly researched document. It's at best a forgery, at worst a grotesque manifesto for society's ruin. Never has the judge laid eyes on such a vile, pernicious and dishonest story. A story of such dubious provenance that it will surely damn the defendant before the trial has even begun. The defence barrister approaches the bench with all the solemnity they can muster. He fixes his thumbs into his dusty black robes and wraps his fingers on his puffed-out chest. He rocks back and forth on the balls of his feet and fixes the judge with a twinkling eye. And then he just hums. He laughs and then he hums.

×

Dizzi and I are in the rhododendrons. My oldest and dearest co-conspirator. A fellow apprentice and time traveller. We met in a sandpit at the age of three, both engaged in our own nefarious acts, the details of which it would not be appropriate to disclose here as it might prejudice the outcome of this criminal trial. We had immediately recognized each other as fellow explorers. The pioneer bond. A bond of blood. A bond that spanned across time. A bond instantly sealed. Today we are waiting for Commander Stuber to receive his latest delivery from the mothership. It could be spare parts for his ray weapon or another batch of that elixir he seems so fond of. Or maybe a brown paper package containing his special books. You never can tell what it will be. That's what I tell Dizzi. He nods in agreement. It's getting dark. That hazy twilight between *Doctor Who* and bedtime. Soon my mother will call us for tea. Oven-ready lasagne and peas. Earlier in the day we had found fragments of broken pottery while digging in the dirt of my family's suburban garden. These splinters of supermarket dinner plates were like the entrails of a sacrificed cockerel, or bones cast by seers. They held the power of prophecy that only young minds could understand. The splinters divined true intentions. The broken pottery was a message, a marker left by a previous civilisation that had once occupied the fields of Chaffinch-On-The-Hill. The fragments pointed to the landing of an enormous spacecraft on this exact spot many aeons ago. Furthermore, they suggested that the Stuber family at number 3 were the advance guard of an alien battle fleet, space scientists sent from the outer galaxies to study humanity. The stains on the Stuber's creosoted fence also suggested the comings and goings of interplanetary vehicles. The family themselves hid their alien natures well. They dressed in traditional Earth clothes. Nylon. Easy iron shirts and action slacks. They had unremarkable haircuts and drove reliable cars. Plus they had strange accents. My dad said they were German, but we knew better. I caught a hint of Venusian in the rolling Rs. Herr Stuber worked for a spectacles manufacturer. Frau Stuber was a teacher. Human jobs taken to mask their true intentions. They were a very nice family but needed to be monitored. With the help of my binoculars – a recent birthday gift – Dizzi and I could see them moving about in their kitchen, pretending to eat Earth food and drink Earth beverages, Herr Stuber occasionally glancing out of the window, waiting for a scout ship to land.

My mum was calling from the front door. The lasagne had reached boiling point, and the peas were popping in the pan. Insects had begun to mock our static boy bodies. Buzzing, diving and nipping. Surveillance was becoming uncomfortable. Dizzi's stomach rumbled. Mine too. We were about to abandon our mission when a tremendous gust of wind rattled the stems of the bush where we were hiding and caused the grass of the Stuber's lawn to sway violently. The gust turned into a gale. The gale to a whirl-wind. Our anoraks rustled and our hair swept into our wide eyes. All around us trees and hedges strained in the gathering tornado. Then came the sound of engines. Not the roar of a jet or the chug of a train but a deep sonorous drone. Lights began to skitter across the deciduous borders. Multicoloured beams stuttering across the spectrum. Disco lights. A craft of alien origin descended in a perfectly ver-tical trajectory. Its hull was invisible to all save Dizzi and I and Commander Stuber, of course. It was shaped like a por-table barbeque, with three telescopic legs jutting from the bottom. It settled silently on the lawn just shy of the gazebo and the stone fountain water feature. A hatch opened. Herr Stuber had exited the patio door and was making his way across the lawn to where the craft hummed expectantly. He climbed the ramp that had glided silently from the hatch and disappeared inside the vessel.

My mum was listing the ingredients of dessert now, hoping to entice us both to return to the safety of home. Custard and crumble. Stomachs groaned. Just one more minute. Suddenly Herr Stuber appeared. He emerged from out of the hatch. His whole body was covered in a fine sticky mucus. He held an object in his slimy palms. Dizzi grabbed my binoculars and focused in on the object. He gasped and shook his head, a look of confusion on his face. He handed me the binoculars. I peered and adjusted the focus. I could make out a square shape, thin, about 30 centimetres in diameter. There was writing on it. At first I took the characters to be alien hieroglyphs, but Dizzi thought it might be human writing. He was right. There were words. And there was an image too. Four humans inside a vehicle. A flying vehicle. The figures had landed. Like prophets descending from heaven. Dizzi wrote the words down on a scrap of paper for us to decipher later. My mum was becoming increasingly agitated as the lasagne was beginning to lose its healthy glow. We shrugged as the space vehicle took off in its perfectly vertical trajectory and Herr Stuber closed the sliding patio door. As we ran back to my house, we thought we could hear the sound of our future drifting across the Stuber's lawn from the inside of the capsule. Later, as the custard congealed in our bowls, we studied the field notes we had made. There were only two words on the scrap of paper. Abba. Arrival. This was how rock and roll arrived in Chaffinch-On-The-Hill.

3

Crossing the weird interzone

Chaffinch-On-The-Hill lies in that mysterious interzone between town and country where concrete melts into mud and exhaust fumes cake the trunks of trees on the ragged border. It's a land of bypasses, litter and laybys. Piles of porn in woody dells, abandoned white goods and rusting vans. It's a province of thwarted ambition where half-realised architectural projects flounder under the weight of nimbyism and council corruption. Poorly executed town centres focused on sixties utopian concrete structures that sit awkwardly next to twee thatched pubs of a similar vintage but with a different vision of the future. Dull conservatism blended with the blunt edge of brutalism. But away from the confusion of human design there is a rebellious landscape full of hidden signs.

Hemmed in between A roads, an insolent woodland blossoms. The home of the rat, fox and vole. Spindly branches arch over the dull black highways like the wizened arms of witches, while their roots subvert the tarmac. Green living in difficult times. Rural Mod rules. Down these shady lanes ride the Chaffinch Rucking Machine on their underpowered motorcycles, their jarring engines cutting across the muted sound of birdsong with their fizzing whine. Even out here in the liminal borderland youth cults flourished; Eggerton Mods, The Fuxbridge Mind Robbers, Wycombe Skins, Lower Banforth Boot Boys. Most were harmless. There was some Thunderbird wine consumed in bus shelters and a lot of spit, but they still helped old ladies with their shopping. The CRM. Formerly known as the Chaffinch Wrecking Machine until someone pointed out that 'wrecking' was spelt with a W and not an R, and so if they were to persist with the name they would have to diligently edit all the local graffiti. So, rucking it was. In practice they rarely caught anyone or administered any punishment beatings because their underpowered engines acted like warning sirens, scattering their victims long before they came in sight. Only as their squeaking row recedes, the concerns of humanity are forgotten, and the chatter of insects replaces the mechanical hum.

It is now 1977 and I'm scrambling down the bank that leads to the Lower Road. I have already crossed the forest of Rouge Mount. A strip of land barely four metres wide dotted with a few shrubs and one fir tree. To young eyes this was a jungle of inscrutable density. But as limbs lengthened and wisdom was extended, the limits of this kingdom were revealed. As I ventured further in I realised this meagre strip was only a foretaste of the world that lay beyond the Lower Road's asphalt boundary. Through a gap in the fence, I could see the folds of a mighty forest, its interior dark with the promise of adventure. Trees with improbable structures to climb. Camps to build from their discarded limbs. I learnt patience and waited for the courage to escape the watchful eye of my parents. The years multiplied and brought with them increased freedom. Don't go too far. Make sure you are home for tea.

These were the 1970s, a decade careless of the hazards lurking in the outside world. A decade before pin drops and location finders, before mobile phones, before satellite navigation and parental guidance advised. This was the decade of television appeals and search parties. The decade of sticks prodding the earth, of discarded clothing and sandals, of nameless terrors and stranger danger. Into this darkness I scrambled. Down the leaf strewn bank. Past the skinny arms of grey saplings draped with flags of discarded crisp packets. Past the ancient cider bottles partly digested by the soil. Past the carrion left by speeding cars, here on the bank where animals staggered to die, clipped by Allegro bumpers and the tires of the Talbot Sunbeam. I was on the edge. The road was like a river too wide to jump, too deep to ford. I paused. On the other bank I could see the enticing flotsam of fly tipping. Boxes and bags, old suitcases, twisted furniture. Magazines. There was the promise of enlightenment in this slowly mouldering library. But first I must cross the barrier.

The Green Cross Code. That catechism recited by the man who would be Vader. Stop. Look. Listen. Think. Socratic wisdom spoken by a muscle-bound superhero and his occasional robot sidekick. David Prowse, Bristolian body builder and later actor, the chosen messenger of British road safety. Stop. Look. Listen. Think. Simple empiricism. The analytic mind of UK government displayed in tight green leggings. But Prowse and the mind of government missed the complex ontology of road safety. Here on the edge, I could see there was more to crossing the road than the Green Cross Code man was letting on. The road was a gateway to another dimension. All roads were. Here on the edge, I could see the tangled lattice of time lanes and the shifting silhouette of a thousand different outcomes as the multiverse danced before my eyes. It is only the young, the psychedelically rearranged and the dedicated demon who can see this bewildering web. David Prowse could not.

This was the Lower Road. A thin strip of tarmac. A psychic barrier that, once crossed, could never be navigated the same way again. I placed my foot cautiously on the hard surface. Stop! My foot recoiled like a snake striking in reverse as a Vauxhall Cavalier shot past on its way to the bypass. I had forgotten the first, second and third rules of the Green Cross Code. Stop. Look. Listen. Think. I stopped. Time froze. Even insects hung static in the cool air of the lane. I looked. Left. Right. Nothing. An emptiness like the cold void of space occupied the horizon. I listened. I could hear an unstructured symphony. A cascade of notes playing up and down the scale in every conceivable pattern until it merged into one continues tone. That single note. The note of all notes vibrated down the road, filling every corner of the wood. Every cell of my body shook with the hum. I looked back up the bank to the gap in the rusty old fence. But it was too late to turn back now. Think. But this was no time to rationalise; it was time to do. I stepped onto the Lower Road and walked like Jesus on the lake. Every step brought me a new kind of joy. I was happier than I had ever been. Maybe this was what it was like to be alive. I was free of the orbit of my family. Free from school and homework and doing the washing up, free from bedtime and wash your hands before tea, free of growing pains and the decaying ache of arthritis, free of bad bowl haircuts, free of male pattern baldness, free of birth, free of death. I was timeless and at one with the tarmac and trees. Step by step towards nowhere. Towards no-when. As my tennis pumps touched the soft soil on the far side, the ground seemed to carry me into a different orbit. Everything was changing. Synapses snapped into new alignments. I glanced back across the road and saw a small boy at the top of the slope gazing wide-eyed through a gap in the rusty fence. I realised I would never see that innocent boy again. He dissolved and died, passing back into the flow.

As the past dissolved, so the future condensed. A punk rock and roller cycled by on a clapped-out chopper. He sneered at me with a curled lip, just like the ones on television. He had food dye in his hair, and he seemed to be annoyed at everything for some reason. I'd recently witnessed the Sex Pistols on the Grundy show and recognized one of their fellow travellers. He had written 'Sid Vicious for Pope' on the back of his old school blazer in Tipp-Ex. I thought he looked nice, so I waved. He flicked the Vs at me and cycled on. I kicked at the discarded cans in the layby like a punk. Old oil tins and Pepsi cola. I wrinkled my brow at the weird square wrappers and used condoms thrown from the windows of two litre Rovers during late-night clandestine trysts. I often noticed the searching beams of car headlights from my bedroom window, scanning the wooded lane in the twilight hours before bedtime. Two vehicles. Two lovers. Car beams cut. Parked up in the layby. The slam of doors in the night. Steam and rocking suspension. The discarded things looked like the exoskeletons of space worms. That was it. They were among us. I looked into a few of the soggy boxes. Domestic crap mainly. Old plastic bottles of Nivea and broken tools. A mattress, of course. An office chair with one wheel missing. Good for games of Davros. I pushed it, but it just stuck in the dirt and fell over. Just like the Daleks. I was Doctor Who. A rolled-up carpet. With a body rolled up inside. No. Just a rat that soon scurried off into the undergrowth. I kicked another box. It gave off a solid thud. I peered in. Sunday supplements. One had a nice-looking lady on the cover. I took it out and imagined she was my mum. I'd be proud to have such a nice-looking mum, I thought. All the grown-up men seemed to put a high premium on nice-looking ladies. Perhaps I could join in the saucy banter which peppered all good drinks party in the 1970s. To be honest, it all seemed odd to me. Like growling lions in polyester slacks. I didn't really understand. Everything was artifice with those cats. Some magazines about cars. The connection between objects made explicit. Nice-looking ladies on nice-looking cars. This was puzzling. All the ladies I knew would never be so stupid as to sit on a car. You might dent the bonnet, or the car might roll off unexpectedly. Plus they were dressed for swimming, not driving. Men were ridiculous, even on the cusp of nine I knew that. Some magazines about nature and the Canadian tundra. *National Geographic*. Digging down deeper where the heat of decay hit its keenest note, here were some very odd artifacts. The covers again depicted ladies, but these ladies did not seem to be smiling and happy like the supplement ladies. They appeared to be either surprised, in pain or caught unawares. They were mainly naked. The writing was funny too. To the untrained eye it would have looked like gibberish, but to a highly trained spy like me they made perfect sense. I immediately recognized the alien hieroglyphics of Commander Stuber's native Venusian. These must be his special books. I quickly opened them. He had made a terrible error, soon the Venusian battle plans would be revealed, and the Earth would be saved. The Venusian battle plans flopped open, their crinkled pages flapping in the cool breeze of the lane. Dear mother of God! These were not the diagrams I had been expecting. So, this is what Commander Stuber had in store for humanity. Some form of wrestling contest. I quickly returned the battle plans to the box. It would be many years before I could decipher their meaning; even now I'm not sure I will ever fully understand.

My initial studies of the decaying stash had been disconcerting and only mildly enlightening. But the border had now been breached and I was in the forest, so I decided to press on into its dark heart. It was a labyrinth of dancing shadows beyond anything I had thought possible. A variety of wild plant life made mockeries of order, exploding in dramatic clumps, weaving between trunks like angry spaghetti. The air smelt of life. Decay, fox piss and nettle blossom. Dog shit rose in occasional curling piles. There was a path made by the feet of their human companions. Stumbling through the thicket, thwacking away with broken twigs like lost Chindits. This was the home of the unruly roots. Man had no dominion here. Neither did small boys. I ran through the woods, letting the stems of the plants whip my face and hands. Sap, cobwebs and the sting of thorns. This was a penitent's path to the timeless core. Young eyes see beyond simple measurements. Older eyes heavy with woe and cynicism would later calculate the wood to be no more than two hundred meters across and perhaps four hundred meters in length. But in 1977, right here, right now, it was a dimensionless landscape of infinite wonder.

I followed the path into the density. There were dells and dips, surrounded by trees with arms like tentacles. I picked up a fallen stick that looked like a musket. I ran up and down the incline firing wildly with my flintlock. The stick became a ray weapon, the trees the pirate raiders from the galaxy of greed. We engaged in good-natured slaughter until the sweat stained the fabric of my aertex shirt. In places the young branches of saplings arched and bowed to form low canopies like a tepee. I crouched under their shade and drew plans in the dirt with my musket ray stick. Ants colonised the trenches I had made. Time collapsed in the forest; its passing was nearly impossible to determine. But by the lengthening of the shadows and the subtle chill, I could tell it was getting late. For all I knew I could have been in there for hours, possibly days. I calculated that I could most likely survive indefinitely here within the forest on the bounty it offered. Blackberries.

Discarded supermarket ready meals past their sell-by dates. Road kill. But my mother's cooking was preferable, and tonight she had promised savoury pancakes and beans. I tried to retrace my steps but soon realised that I was hopelessly lost. Everything was trunks and roots. Directions became impossible to discern. Dimensions too. This place seemed endless, just like the universe. No centre. No terminus. I wandered back down a lonely path that wound its way through the dark thicket. I carelessly struck out at the leaves with my musket ray stick, humming a song I'd heard on the radio. Take me home, country road.

A Mixtape for Crossing the Weird Interzone

Side One

1. *Yes, It's – The Clovers*
2. *Silent Street/Silent Dub – Maximum Joy*
3. *I'm So Glad – The Fuzz*
4. *Bible Story – Early B*
5. *Do You Really Know How I Feel – Jimmy & Vella*
6. *You and Me – Solaris*
7. *I Am Drum – Reuben*
8. *Baltimore Oriole – Lorez Alexandria*
9. *Devil Go – David Waciuma Rapture Voices*
10. *Good For You, Good For Me – Sunburst*
11. *Are You Glad to Be in America? – James Blood Ulmer*

12. *Third World – Paladin*

13. *Call of the Drums - Johnny and the Attractions*

Side Two

1. *Free Wheel – Hard Meat*

2. *Ain't No Love in the Heart of the City – Barrett Strong*

3. *Launderette – Vivien Goldman*

4. *Waiting – Harem*

5. *Peace and Love – Brooklyn People*

6. *Trash That Blad – Animal Magic*

7. *Angie La La – Nora Dean*

8. *Falling In and Out of Love – Johnny Nash*

9. *All of Your Life – Shirley Nanette*

10. *Flicker – The Flying Lizards*

11. *Entente Africaine – D'Almeida Blucky et Les Black Santiago de Cotonou*

12. *Inside America – Juggy Murray Jones*

13. *Civilisation in the World – Bright Engelberts*

4

the PiPe of God

Pools of purple shadow spread and merged to form a sopo-rific wash of twilight tones. Evening had come to the wood, and I was lost. The path seemed to lead nowhere in particu-lar; it just wound round and round the ever-changing maze of shrubs. Panic would have been appropriate. But I felt quite calm. The possibility I was facing certain death didn't bother me too much. I felt at home and free. My mind could wander and form new connections to dimensions adults could no longer reach. Even before I entered the clearing I knew I was not alone. Beyond the wood spirits, the animals and insects, there was the unmistakable crackle of presence. The path opened up from out of the close tunnel of stems into a cool glade, lit like a stage by the weak shafts of light cast by the dying sun. There was an unnatural symmetry to the space. In contrast to the unstructured wildness of the surrounding wood, the perimeter of the glade was an almost perfect circle. Leaves, wood chip and twigs were all laid out in the same direction, as if whirled flat by a giant centrifuge. It reminded me of my mother's whisked cream desserts topped with crumbled chocolate and sprinkled with nuts. At the centre of the spiral of leaves was an old oak tree, knobbly and crooked, its bark corrupted by lichen and elegant toadstool growths. It looked ancient and wise. Around the bottom of the trunk a faint mist swirled. A scent caught my attention. It was sweet-smelling smoke dancing in the shafts of light. The smoke was rising from the bowl of a pipe. The pipe, a finely carved horn like the one favoured by Sherlock Holmes in Sidney Paget's illustrations, was dangling from the lips of an old woman. The old woman was sitting on the woodland floor, leaning against the trunk with her legs jutting out at ninety degrees, her feet swaying to and fro in time to some silent tune like characters in a puppet show. She was staring at me. There was something about her eyes, two dark pools, that drew me towards their orbit. I entered the clearing. Her features became clearer. She was both staggeringly beautiful and staggeringly old. Her deep, ebony-toned face was angular with pronounced cheekbones set off by a proud dome of thick grey hair. Her skin was patterned with wrinkles that suggested wisdom rather than wear. She was full-bodied with a robust frame. Taut with no excess flesh. Her hands, elegant and aquiline, came to a point at the tip of some extraordinarily long talons. One cupped the bowl of the pipe, the other beckoned me closer with a graceful motion of the index finger. I moved as if pulled along by invisible strings. Closer. Closer. I tilted my head in puzzled inquiry. In this monocultural backwater, it was unusual to see anyone other than the whitest of white folk, so someone of such notable appearance would have elicited whispers and gossip amongst my neighbours. I was acutely tuned to these types of communications and had detected no mention of an elegant woman of colour smoking a pipe in any recent chats across the garden fence. Perhaps she was new? I thought I had better introduce myself and find out.

'Hello, who are you? My name's Jo—'

'Jonah, yes, I know who you are young man. Come and sit here next to me.'

Her voice was as elegant as her appearance, commanding without being censorious, soothing and yet powerful. Her tone shifted effortlessly through the keys from baritone to alto. Her accent was impossible to place, at once a 'sophisticated countess' with an air of finishing school truant and, simultaneously, a venerable grandmother imparting homespun wisdom on the stoop. She patted the ground with her long, taloned hand. I shuffled across the neat carpet of leaves and sat down next to her. She smiled at my crinkled-up face that was racked with questions.

'How do you know my name?' My small brow knitted harder together.

'I know all, and I know nothing, Jonah.'

This, on the face of it, seemed an impossible assertion. But from her lips the statement took on an air of certainty. I nodded and my brow relaxed a little. I let my small sandaled feet sway in time to the rhythm of hers. For a few seconds we were both silent, watching our feet move this way and that. I became aware of her penetrating gaze, her eyes tunnelling into me, searching for the cracks in my developing consciousness.

'What's your name then? You know mine, and it seems fair that I should know yours, so we can be friends.'

'Friends?'

She sounded surprised, perhaps annoyed. I began to feel uneasy. I had been terribly presumptuous. But a smile gradually formed on her face and her exquisite hand patted my head sympathetically. I smiled in relief.

'Friends, yes. OK, Jonah, if you like, though you might not find what I have to say to your liking. You see, I have a task for you.'

This sounded depressingly like homework. My shoulders sagged. And she still hadn't even told me her name. It didn't seem fair to hand out chores without first telling a boy your name. I pressed her again with just the faintest hint of impatience.

'Yes, but what is your name? I would very much like to know what to call you, miss.'

'Yes, yes, alright! You are such an impatient species, Christ. Now let me think.'

She took a long puff on her pipe, blowing out a plume of smoke that looked like a dragon in flight slowly dissolving in the thick woodland air. Now it was her brow that was furrowed. She muttered to herself, her lips quivering as she searched for the correct answer. Our eyes met. Suddenly she waved her pipe in excitement.

'God! Yes, that's what you call me. God! It's been a while since I was known by that name, but hey, here we are. You can call me God. Short, snappy, easy to remember.'

I nodded slowly and considered running. I eyed the escape routes, but there were none. Even the path by which I had entered had been swallowed up and smoothed into an impenetrable wall of branches and leaves. God sensed my unease.

'What on Earth are you worried about, Jonah? I'm not going to smite you or do whatever nonsense you've read about me in books. Pillars of salt and all that jazz. I don't go in for that sort of thing. In fact, I'd never even heard of mankind until about an hour ago. Not that I deal with hours you understand, but well, I'm just giving you a rough timescale that you might understand, get it?'

I didn't get it. God was not supposed to be like this. I pressed her on the details. 'But didn't you make us? I mean, didn't you make everything? That's what all the books say, and at school we've even got a song about it we sing at assembly: "All things bright and—"'

Her hand shot to close my mouth as my angelic voice crackled out the tune. 'Stop! Stop! That fucking song.' Now she really was annoyed. The grove swirled with a violent tornado as leaves and branches were sucked up into an angry vortex. Then, as suddenly as it had started, it stopped. She looked embarrassed. 'Sorry. Forgive my language, kid. Just forget what I said. It's just I'm not a fan, understand? No, look, the thing is, I didn't make shit. The void is more my scene. You know nothingness?'

I had no idea what she was talking about. She was switching from school teacher to street poet, from governess to sweet sibling. Her diction was flowing across time and space. She paused and scratched her scalp through her thick hair.

'How can I break this to you? OK, look at all this stuff here.' She pointed at the trees, the sky, the dead leaves. 'This I knew about. I mean, I didn't make it, the kids did, but I did at least see the plans, but you …' And here she poked me gently with her long nail. 'You I had nothing to do with. God made man in his image. Isn't that what it says? Ridiculous! I mean this outfit looks pretty good, right?' She indicated her features. 'But this isn't me, this is just a manifestation, like the burning bush but with a pair of sneakers.' She wiggled her feet which were now shod in box-fresh trainers. 'I am formless, timeless, the ground of all being. And certainly, better dressed. But all that will have to wait. I have something I'd like you to do for me.'

I nodded, trying to appear as if I understood. I was proud that God had chosen me for this task, whatever it was. She looked at me in a way that suggested she was unsure if she had chosen her agent unwisely.

'I'm much happier in the void and don't appreciate spending time down here with all this stuff, but even I make mistakes. Boredom. That's something basic in all things. It's ever-present. Like God, boredom just *is*. There is boredom in the void too. The void is lonely. I should have absorbed it and used it. But boredom got the better of me. So, I made some companions. Dogs. Cats. Parrots. Demons. Dogs were cool, but demons, now they were a mistake. Nice enough to begin with but always taking liberties. They started making things of their own. Kids like to mimic, you know. They saw their mother making dogs and parrots and before too long they were filling the nursery with their own creations. Thing is, they never stuck to the plans. They were forever cutting corners, using cheap materials, drinking on the job, generally fucking about when they should be concentrating on the task in hand. To be honest, Jonah, I'm not sure why they made anything. The emptiness is far more rewarding. Did I fail them as a mother?'

Her voice dropped to a conspiratorial murmur. She looked wistful. God was whispering in my ear. 'My life would have been so much easier if demons had stuck to nothingness, like me, you know, the family trade. I'd long given up on creation, but the demons really seemed to like it. After mimicry comes rebellion. Kids like to go off in alternative directions. The opposites apply, so if we are going to have nothing we had better have something too. I suppose I shouldn't be annoyed. They were young and bored, just like me when I was young. This is how the material world came to be. Beer cans, potato peelers, taxation, mandatory forms, sprinklers, the wheel, haemorrhoid cream and guitar strings. The demons made them. Tinkering in the garage after school. They made them, sent them out into the world and then let them go about their business – and that was all fine. I indulged them like all parents do. I smiled as they showed me their latest creations, no matter how grotesque. But soon their creations became more sophisticated and more sinister. Gone were the useful nick-nacks and pretty things. The workshop was turning out darker materials. Shoulder holsters, box junctions, amusing curly straws, pestilence, operator hold music, single-use vapes, substandard glue, greed, guilt, revolving doors, roadside explosive devices, unbalanced benches, wire coat hangers, Thames Water Authority and unrollable posters. All this consumer shit. And humans. That's when I decided to intervene. Humans. I cannot let that pass. There is something wrong with humans. A smudge on the blueprint. They are like the teenage party that ends in vomit and recriminations. Paranoid. Truculent. Faulty. Dangerous. It's fucking things up and making a mess. I can't sleep with all the horror. So here I am trying to work out what to do about it. That's where you might come in.'

I adopted the serious face I'd seen my father make when he was talking about work. God was talking about us. 'Are you saying we're a mistake? Is that what you're saying? A mistake made by demon force?'

She looked thoughtful. She puffed on her pipe before considering her answer. 'Yup, that's about the size of it. Santo was the first. He's the one you should blame. Handsome chap, good with his hands, but prone to making rash judgements. Hates being told what to do. Maaaan, the times I had to summon him before my presence to ask him to explain himself. Fucking Santo, what a pain in the arse. Satan is what you lot round these parts call him, but you could just as well call him daddy.'

God chuckled to herself. Her laugh was like refreshing rain on parched ground. But I had no reason to laugh. I was a son of Satan. We all were. I began to cry. The hymns were all wrong. God held my tear-stained face in her hand and, looking more serious now, she continued.

'Look, I'm sorry to break it you like that, son. I'm not a vengeful God, not like they say in the scriptures. To be frank, I'm more of an absent parent. But I would absolutely hate to wipe you all out of existence. Santo's not a bad kid, he's just secretive. I wished he'd introduced us earlier. It's just I know so little about you, and before you ask, 'all knowing' was another exaggeration. Sure, I'm a quick learner, that's how I know your names, but really I know nothing, Jonah. I mean that literally, no-thing-ness, that's me. Always around but never found. There's a human-shaped gap in the mind of God and I'm here to fill it. You might be able to help.'

I considered her offer. Death or life. 'Well, I'd love to help you out if I could, if you don't mind working with the spawn of Satan.'

Now we both chuckled. Her dark eyes met mine and she ruffled my hair again.

'You're alright for a demon. The task is quite simple. The question simpler still. Why are you, Jonah? Not just you, but anybody. I'm trying to take an interest in my kid's hobbies. I'm trying to be a better mother. The last thing I want to do is to take his toys away and be forced to throw you all in the recycling. What is it about your species that young Satan finds so fascinating? That's all I want to know, Jonah. What makes you tick. Call it a gnostic quest if you like. Or perhaps a defence in a criminal trial. You'll need evidence if you don't want me to pass a harsh sentence. I need mitigation. I need reasons not to stamp you into the dust. I need testimonies of ecstasy. I need to find a soul in the guts of the beast. Look on it as an expedition. A trip fraught with peril and pleasure. I want you to suck the marrow out of life itself. I want you to bleed life dry. Because in the blood is the code. In the sap, the message. I need data so that I can assess your relative suitability for continued existence. No pressure, of course. There's no time limit beyond your own, somewhat truncated, lifespan. I don't expect all the answers. Who the fuck has them? I just want to join you in the conversation. God. Humanity. We're related. Like you said, let's try and be friends, and if we can't, well, then I promise to make the end as painless as possible. It's up to you. Make the case. Go out into the world, young Jonah, and report your findings.'

'OK,' I answered. 'Will I need any special equipment?' I was hoping for some James Bond-like gadgets, perhaps a digital watch that turned into a submarine.

'Sure. I mean, everyone has all the tools they need really, it's just that few choose to use them correctly. But I'll lay a few powers on you to help you on your way. Suckers are cool, you can deploy them when needed; they're neat and fold away like wings. But I will warn you, things could get messy. This isn't a job for the squeamish. There will be blood. You must infiltrate the highest echelons of your chosen trade. I need to know what a successful life might look like, but I need the depths, too, so you'll need to wallow in the mire for a time, pick up some bad habits, maybe get up to no good on both ends of the spectrum. Ambition. Get some of that, that's bound to lead to disappointment. Rock and roll I recommend as a trade. It's as close to heaven as you'll ever get. I've had lots of good feedback from rock and rollers. You might be forced into depravity, that's good, don't fight it, feel it. You might also find yourself on the wrong side of the law, but don't sweat it. "Do what thou wilt", as an old acquaintance of mine once put it. Just make sure you're up for the challenge. Time is often an issue with your species, so I'm going to let you play about with it for a bit. It'll be fun. Well, most of the time, but I have to tell you, being reborn is no joke. You will need to feed.'

God paused and fixed me with a serious stare. 'All good fiends must feed, and make no mistake, you are a fiend. You will feel the urge to suck the life out of, well, life. Do not resist. Give in to your desires. Whatever they are. I'm a bit sketchy on the details, but I'm led to believe by some of my spies that it is desire that will sustain you. The urge will make you do things you may find awkward but not altogether unpleasant. So, if you don't fancy breaking a few eggs to make an omelette, you'd best back out now and we'll say no more about it.'

This was all just a list of bewildering words. I had no idea what a gnostic quest might be or what constituted data, plus the idea of bloodletting sounded unpleasant, but I was fond of omelettes, so… I offered my hand to shake in agreement. God spat in her palm to seal the deal. I drizzled my own spit onto my hand, and we shook on it. The touch of her fingers was like touching eternity; I could feel every atom in the universe flowing through her wizened hand. There was warmth and comfort and joy. I closed my eyes and let the bliss of God baptise every cell in my body. I felt a vague tingle as my vampire suckers were woven into my skin, a slight jolt as my new powers were enhanced inside my cortex. I was reborn and renamed. Son of a Demon

God. When I opened my eyes, she was gone. Not even a shadow remained. There was no glade, no perfect woodland circle, only the faint ribbon of a poorly lit B road and the hulks of discarded household objects littered in the layby.

On my way home I came across a small suitcase, the type a teenage girl might pick out for her first trip abroad. It had been damaged by the damp but somehow I knew it was only freshly abandoned. None of the usual dead leaves and dirt had gathered around it, as was common with older woodland objects. I opened it and studied the contents. Neatly folded clothing of an adolescent weave. A hairbrush still clinging to a few strands of brown hair. A nightgown dotted with holes where the mites had begun to burrow. There was a book. An exercise book, just like the ones we used at school. On the cover was a quite skilful rendering of a pop band's logo. Abba. Arrival. Under the logo in block capitals. MY DIARY. PRIVATE. KEEP OUT! God's first gift was suspicion. Her second was a disregard for privacy. I opened the book. The words spoke of a dormant horror stirring:

Today he gave me a lift home from school. I think he likes me. A+. He thinks I'm gifted. He asked me to help him after class setting up scenery for the school play. Our hands touched. No one understands, but he does. I don't need anyone else. Our first kiss. He loves me. We are going to run away together. Tonight. Tonight

is the night. I'll climb out the window when they are
all asleep. I love him and he loves me. I can't wait for
the future. We will be so happy. A childish heart and a
smiley face.

There the text stopped. I filed my first report for God and
went home for pancakes and beans.

Mixtape for God

Side One

1. Like an Angel Passing Through My Room – Abba

2. God's Garden – John J. Francis

3. God Made Me Funky – The Headhunters

4. Heaven – Dennis Bovell

5. Dancing Gods – Silver Apples

6. God of Claws – Mzylkypop

7. God-Box – The Fall

8. Goddess Atonement – Six Organs of Admittance

9. The Sun God – Wyld Olde Souls

10. Temptation 'Bout to Get Me – Knight Brothers

11. The Message – Gyedu-Blay Ambolley

12. The Kingdom Within You – Ira Sullivan

13. Airline to Heaven – Wilco

Side Two

1. *Heavenly Dub – Culture*
2. *Heaven is Being with You – Jackie DeShannon*
3. *Gettin' High for Jesus – Holly Golightly & The Brokeoffs*
4. *Buddha Knows – Sondi Sodsai*
5. *Mojn Buddha – George Kranz*
6. *Temple of Convenience – Yeah Yeah Noh*
7. *Ah Ji Wah Wah: Selam Nna Wadada (Peace & Love) – Count Ossie & The Mystic Revelation of Rastafari*
8. *Church Yard – Odyssey*
9. *Praise the Lord – Mary Lou Williams*
10. *It is Right to Give Drones and Praise – Tau & the Drones of Praise*
11. *Give Thanks and Praise – Barry Brown*
12. *La Danza De Kali – Rada*
13. *In My Time of Dying (Jesus Make Up My Dying Bed) – Blind Willie Johnson*

5

red
wellington
boots and
the birth
of disco

I'm rattling around between snare and kick drum. Bouncing between notes. *I wanna see all my friends at once.* I'm in the basement of the Roadhouse. I'm in the Electric Chair; the Unabombers are playing Arthur Russell jams. *I want to see all my friends at once.* Here they are, every last one of them. I haven't slept for days. I've got speed from 1982, Es from '88, mushrooms from the dawn of time. *I wanna see all my friends at once.* Some are headbanging in cut-off denim vests. Some are doing the chicken dance. Some are dancing around maypoles hoping for a good harvest. All my friends are here, even the ones I don't really like. Bullies from school, the guy who nicked my Sabres acetate from the booth at Mirage, the taxi driver looking for fairs in my living room at 5am, the copper with his little notepad taking names after busting a rave in a field off the M62. Dinosaurs roam the earth. I was friendly with a herd of Triceratops in the late Cretaceous; they are trance dancing on the speaker cabinets. Dinosaur L. Dinosaur love. Rat-a-tat-tat. Someone's knocking at the door, somebody ringing the bell. I'm in the tour bus with the resurrected Beatles; we've wrapped their resurrected tour manager in toilet paper like an Egyptian mummy. Macca is playing demos, manically swapping cassettes in the machine. This is Wings. Like flight. Woosh. We are high as balls. We've been listening to George Russell's *Electronic Sonata* for 24-hours straight. Rat-a-tat-tat. There's that sound again. I've got my eyes closed; the Unabombers just dropped a Staple Singers spiritual number into the mix – it's fucking spectacular. Lennon loses it; he's running around the Roadhouse naked as the day he was born. The dinosaurs are scoring blues. Some of my friends are wearing thrift store threads and trying to quote Oscar Wilde. But no one can hear them in the beautiful din. *I wanna see all my friends at once.* I'm wearing a black polo-neck jumper, Prince of Wales check strides and black patent leather Chelsea boots. I'm channelling Napoleon Solo and Savalas' *On Her Majesty's Secret Service*. Techno breakbeat modernism. The heat is intense. It's beautiful too. The air in the basement is full of the particles of people mingling in the soundwaves. The Unabombers play Hi Tech Jazz. Lennon and McCartney decide on a whole new direction. Rat-a-tat-tat. There's that nagging noise again. Someone get that door will ya? Ringo does the honours. He turns and shrugs. Oh, fuck, it's the cops.

Duration, change and the passing of time. It's difficult. For us time travellers, time exists all at once in an eternal now. Wisdom only diminishes rather than grows with age; all those extra years add is a certain ennui to the back end of life. But for me, everything occurred in a strange present. That's why writing confessions is so difficult, because when I was alive, separating one event from another in any kind of intelligible sequence was a problem. Now that I'm dead it's all much more straightforward. People don't realise that time travel requires a degree of dedication and careful meditation. You can't just rush into it. Not that one has to have any formal qualifications for time travel; there are no diplomas or prizes given out for it, no grades or hierarchies of skill. Judging one's suitability is really a matter of feeling because feeling is only a formless idea, and an idea is just a cashier's cheque from the bank of feeling. People who try to tell you to trust in reason and not feelings need to go down to the basement full of conscious noise where you can actually see ideas and feelings dancing together in front of the speakers. Another useful tip if you are thinking of getting into time travel: don't worry about intelligence. Or cleverness, or education. You don't need an alphabet of acronyms after your name to be a time traveller. You don't even have to be human. Intelligence is way too meaningless a concept to be relevant to time travel; no one really knows what it is anyway. To be a good time traveller, one must be an effective actor. You have to fit in and mould yourself to the situation so as to avoid detection. This should be easy, as all humans are endowed with an enormous capacity for make believe and deception, if only self-deception. In fact, self-deception is the best sort of deception, because it means you can really occupy the role. We humans are like aspiring film stars, jostling for position in a casting line-up. We just keep on hustling for a bigger and better part. If we can't get the lead then, fuck it, we'll make ourselves the directors of the whole fucking thing. 'Masters of reality' in the words of Sabbath. But we do not create reality. I know that now. We just get it wrong. We do not suck up the wavelengths and turn them into colour or turn sonic ripples into music. All we do is blunder into the world pointing at stuff and giving it names. All we add are myths and metaphors. The temptation of Eve or Gaia's gift to Zeus. This is humanity's great contribution. Stories. With words we add to the cosmic catalogue. Characters, magical beasts, strange lands and haunted landscapes. All these new entities are as real as apples or tables or blades of grass. They are fantastic new layers, magical veneers with symbolic power. Peacocks have beautiful feathers, more splendid than any woven cloth. Human minds add nothing to their grace save the eyes of Argos placed there by Hera. Chameleons' bodies flit across the spectrum of colour carrying photonic crystals under their skin. Our faulty eyes only catch a hint of that spectrum, a tiny slither of a greater wonder. But the Karma Chameleon is something new and wonderful too. A Karma Chameleon gives all the other chameleons that extra swagger they need when they go down the disco.

Why have I interrupted an otherwise sprightly confession with this highly contestable account of human consciousness? There is a time and a place for such matters, and this seems to be neither. Well, it's by way of an explanation of just how difficult psychic crime really is. It isn't a case of pressing my fingers to my temples and concentrating in the manner of a music hall magician or one of those ESP experiments popular in science fiction movies. The world will not bend to our will by thought alone. It requires allies and alliances with the shadowy realm of objects. Projecting one's mind is a *unity* of efforts. One needs to be fit, as even the simplest spell can be as psychically demanding as running a marathon. To possess someone, as I often did, required me to enter them physically too, much like a virus. I was forever trimming and slicing bits of my body off in order to infiltrate blood streams or to enter the temporal flow. Rituals also demanded sacrifice and, when victims were scarce, I was forced to use bits of myself to complete the pact. At times I resembled a pin cushion, or the aftermath of a Sunday carvery joint handled by an amateur butcher. I'm not looking for sympathy, and I'm way beyond forgiveness, but I would hate for you to think any of this was easy. After all, blood must pay with blood.

The summer of 1976 was behind us. That blistering furnace where my childhood died, smothered in a pile of ladybirds that swarmed in super abundance. Sweet sweat and heat stroke. I was still a small boy by human standards. I had been in my ever-changing physical form for only eight years. Before that I was as I am now. Nothing. The summer of 1976, where all temperature records were broken and hosepipes were banned. It felt like 'the day the earth stood still'. Scorched streets and withered parks. Some form of preliminary apocalypse. But as the heat finally subsided, the clouds of ladybirds dissolved into the gathering gloom, and summer gave way to autumn and the rustle of nylon snorkel parkas. Eventually the crisp snows of winter arrived, heralding the childish Eden of Christmas, where the desire for material satisfaction drives youngsters like piranhas around a fisherman's ankles. It was also the time of year where parents get utterly fucked on booze.

Rouge Mount Road was one great temple of pleasure in the winter months and 1976 was to be a vintage year. Our small estate initially comprised of a mere four houses that defying all known laws of logic were numbered in reverse. This was typical of the short-term thinking of developers of the period. Fearing impending nuclear war, they presumed that everything would soon be reduced to a radioactive sludge and therefore adherence to any commonly accepted numerical sequence was unnecessary. It is possible that the street was designed by postmodernists or acid-drenched psychonauts riffing on quantum theory. Our road was the living embodiment of a situationist city, where the bourgeois presumptions of a sequential hierarchy that underpinned the oppressive capitalist system were rejected in favour of a more liberated arrangement. A ludic paradise where 1 could be 4 and 3 could be 2. I lived in the fourth house on the street. Number 1 Rouge Mount Road. As the estate grew, the absurdity of the situation became more apparent. No amount of mathematical chicanery or numerical abstraction could disguise the fact that no house in the middle of a street, in middle England, should bear the number 1 on its door. It blew minds and put postal workers in hospital. It caused comment at the highest levels of local government. But it was too late; the Dadaist prank lived on. The peculiar numbering system did have another revolutionary effect, however. Something more potent than forced collectivisation. It engendered a sense of community. The shared experience of misplaced correspondence was akin to the camaraderie found in the trenches of Passchendaele. Cigarettes lit from smouldering butts as talk turned to lost mail order seeds or Boots the chemist's festive catalogue. As letters were consistently posted through the wrong letterboxes, I was often sent to my neighbours' houses with bundles of bills and postcards, delivering them to their rightful destination. I would return with our mail and, more often than not in the festive season, an invite for Christmas drinks.

In the age leading up to this particular year zero, neighbours' drinks were a form of torture. There were no kids of my age on my street. There was no one to play with or to conspire against. These were the years before my powers had been honed and I was entirely unaware of the potential for mischief that they offered. I was bored. Utterly rigid with tedium. Attempts to climb the furniture or repurpose neighbour's ornaments into characters in a fantastical game were met with hasty rebukes. Jonah. Get off that. Jonah. Put that down. It's not yours to play with. Jonah. I attempted to join in adult conversations, parodying the grown-up stance. Fizzy pop glass cradled like a flute of sparkling wine. Hand rubbing chin, nodding thoughtfully to some drunken opinion on industrial relations or the price of fuel. But no one would engage with my point of view, and I was dismissed with a ruffle of my blond curly hair. But the winter of 1976 changed it all. Rock and roll was here. Every good home now had a radiogram. In fact, they probably always did, but it's just now I began to notice them. Before Abba's *Arrival*, music had been some weird buzzing that my mum put on in the morning as she was buttering the toast. Radio 2 and its saccharine sound bed. Parties, too, were quite static affairs. Whereas living rooms in other parts of the globe had been moving to the hip sound since the 1950s, in Chaffinch-On-The-Hill the festive drinks party had been focussed on chat and heavy drinking. Not even Elvis penetrated the austere shield. No Beatles. No Stones. But Abba cracked it. Fucking disco fever hit hard.

That party in the Stuber's capsule. It had all been so routine. Wine in a box, Watney's Red barrel. Cinzano and sweet, sweet mixers. Chats about the unions and bringing back national service, the expected range of routine prejudices expressed with casual abandon, peppering bad jokes and innuendo. Herr Stuber was taking the usual string of World War Two jibes in his stride; he had been a baby when Hitler came to power and not even out of his first decade when the war ended. The fact that his parents had fled Germany to escape Nazi persecution was lost on almost everyone in the area. He must make amends for all the horrors of war by way of a regular comic drubbing. Achtung! Show me ze papers! I have a new disc to play you, he announced, after a flurry of Colditz puns. Frau Stuber topped up glasses. Nibbles circulated. Commander Stuber of the Third Venusian Intelligence Battalion produced a sleeve from the grey frosted glass cabinet that formed the base of his Bang & Olufsen stereo stack. I recognised the image on the sleeve immediately. It was the object Commander Stuber had carried from the space vessel. My eyes widened in wonder and apprehension He could destroy us all, or perhaps turn us into mindless drones. Was it a gift or a weapon? He reached inside the sleeve and produced a black disc. Dear God, it *was* a weapon! A razor-sharp discus for decapitating the enemies of Venus. It seemed to suck all the light from the room into its obsidian grooves. Herr Stuber opened the lid of the turntable and removed the needle from the Mozart piano concerto that had been rotating harmlessly on the platter. In its place he positioned the alien weapon. The needle made contact. A deceptive acoustic guitar jangled into a discarded folk rock chord progression. It was a song about kissing a teacher. Weird, creepy stuff that made Frau Stuber, a teacher herself, blush and launched a fresh barrage of painful slapstick comments along with the music. But then a beat kicked in. Four to the floor. It was lively and happy. Something began to stir amongst the residents of Rouge Mount Road and their guests. Feet began to tap. But this was only an amuse bouche. The next number, 'Dancing Queen', sealed the covenant between the Venusians and humanity. The whole joint blew up. Man-made fibres became clogged with the sweat of the middle management. The swish of rayon crackled as the cul-de-sac came to life.

To be honest, I was an agnostic when it came to Abba. Music was only beginning to reveal itself to my developing mind. My powers, too, remained obscured. But even at this early stage I detected a middle-of-the-road conservatism in the work of Abba that I found wanting.

Something unconvincing and safe, as if they had taken a subversive medium and turned it against itself. I thought of the flower power revolution and lysergic acid tests. The rumble of freak beat. I thought of Coca Cola teaching the world to sing in pastiche cheesecloth. Worse was yet to come. This was Abba to me: an approximation to youth culture but with a corporate endorsement. There must be something beyond the safety net, some well from which Abba's *Arrival* drank. Something darker and more satisfying. But hey, I was eight years old and high on soda pop, so what the fuck did I know? But its power was undeniable, and that is what any self-respecting energy vampire is attracted to. Power. The briefest crackle as the needle popped into the groove of 'Knowing Me, Knowing You' would produce a sudden spasm of collective energy. Stippled pint pots were put aside, and cheese and pineapple sticks were redeployed as coquettish rapiers, waved in the faces of wives and husbands not their own as they moved with an awkward joy over the shagpile. All talk of three-day weeks and bin strikes was forgotten as the primal need to get down took hold. Abba moved the people. My father had an elegant side step and finger click routine. My mother a kind of jewellery rattling shake. The whole neighbourhood swayed with inelegant grace – and I fed.

The surge of energy given off by these recently converted disco fans was intense. The adults, too, sucked at the flow. Tapping in. Tuning in. There was plenty to spare, and so

I feasted. If Abba could do this to a group of conservative middle-class suburbanites, imagine what heavier vibes could achieve. The spark was smouldering into flame. This was what God had commanded. I was feeding off these people, sucking at the zest their bodies gave off. As they moved together they formed webs of life force, ancient latices of pulsing energy driven by drums. I sucked hard at the flow. I jumped and jived. I ran between the grooving grown-ups. I span on my back until my nylon shirt resembled the pelt of a yeti as fibres of Axminister clung to the fabric. The grown-ups laughed and clapped, encouraging me to ever wilder acrobatics. I was one of them. 'I' is 'we' are 'you' are 'me' and 'we' are all together. United by Abba. United by music.

In the subatomic strata of my body, fissures began to form. As my back span on the carpet, tiny fragments of me separated from my body and began to travel. Into the weave of the carpet, down through the underlay, into the floorboards, into the earth, down past the fragments of broken pottery. Back in time. My brain tuned into the movements of microscopic scouts. Memories formed. Early manifestations of vampiric urges. I could see the rusting hulk of a tractor with a small tousled-haired boy sat awkwardly at the rusted controls, his little legs too short to reach the peddles. On his feet are little red wellington boots that kick and wiggle in the air. His face is furrowed in concentration as he tries to manipulate the knackered levers. A group of ramblers approach and then stop. Two older ladies begin to coo. Ah, how sweet. The boy's mother looks proud but anxious. She doesn't want the ramblers to think she routinely puts her child at risk on abandoned farm machinery. She puts her arms around the boy's waist. He wiggles free in protest at this potential impediment to his freedom. His blond curly hair bounces in the breeze. His bright blue eyes flash defiance at this mother and the gathered adults. He will ride this tractor until it will go no further. Isn't he pretty? Look at his little boots. Blond hair. Blue eyes. Vampire child of demonic descent. The boy is me, and I feed. I suck at the attention the women pay me. I play up for laughs. I kick my feet and make engine noises. I smile a toothless grin. I absorb the human bond and strengthen myself with their love.

6

the sandpit of dreams

Appealing to protected religious practices would not go down well with this solidly secular jury. These were twelve strict rationalists who had moved to the city from their rural backwaters with the express desire to escape exactly the kind of superstitious claptrap the defence team was now trying to offer as mitigation for their client's misdeeds. Missions from God were the preserve of perverts and serial killers. Jonah was, of course, both, and so his defence was entirely plausible. The atmosphere in the court had by this time taken on something of a carnival atmosphere. Drink was taken and people were dancing around mobile telephones repurposed as nightclub sound systems. The judge was being treated for shock in his chambers. The trial continues.

✕

Water-blasted particles of crystalline grit are becoming ingrained in my fingernails. I am digging a trench. My plan is to dig a trench so deep that I can slip my entire body into it with ease and thus render myself invisible. There are two reasons why this course of action seems necessary, and indeed urgent; firstly, it is impossibly hot, and the depths of the cool wet sand will provide relief. Secondly, agents of the Portuguese paramilitary police are almost certain to swoop on my position imminently. I am impossibly high. My manager at this point in time does not earn enough money from my modest endeavours to cover the cost of living and so supplements his earnings by flogging ecstasy pills in and around the Greater London area. We are in Portugal. The year is 1989. We are ambassadors of the new youth craze. We are here to spread love. My manager has in his possession a bulging bag of white capsules which he secreted in his anal passage during our flight over, but which he has subsequently passed and decanted into a fresh, clean vessel. I have eaten a number of the pills. I dig deeper. The golden powdery sand gives way to dark grey silt. Over the lip of the trench the vigorous waves of the Atlantic swell smash into the beach. My friends are listening to blissful acid house sounds through a tiny speaker attached to a Walkman cassette player. Andrew Weatherall, live from the Future. I'm digging in the past. Passing shells of long dead molluscs.

Beer bottle caps. I can hear the whine of sirens. The new youth craze is a criminal enterprise. I dig faster and deeper. So deep that I begin to cross hidden thresholds. On the cassette the Residents segues into Royal House.

Newly equipped with my divine mission, life was beginning to take shape. I began to probe and question my actions and the actions of those around me. I was too young for Bowie on the box, but my chance encounter with the Sex Pistols whilst watching wholesome tea time TV had alerted me to the possibility that the record collections of Rouge Mount Road were lacking a certain bite. Bill Grundy represented the old guard's last stand; like the grey-moustachioed grenadiers of Napoleon's Grande Armée surrounded by the punk rock fusillade, he was mown down in a scattershot of expletives and situationist couture. I'm not sure I liked the sounds, but it felt pleasantly dangerous. To be fair, though my mother feigned outrage, my parents made no move to shut the television off; it was all educational after all. But it was my first clue that the generations were engaged in near-constant warfare, or at least they had been since the teenager became a target for mass consumer exploitation in the post-war years. They had heaped the misery on themselves, these advertising executives flogging their blue jeans and hair pomades. Hepped up on hormones and easy lines of credit, teenagers came roaring out of the traps armed with a music so repulsive to the older generation that attempts were made to ban it. The zazous of wartime France had zoot suits and swing jazz, but it's hard to thrive with a jackboot on your face. The lusty gallants of medieval Europe had bright-coloured hose and heavy lute riffs, but the plague shut down the clubs and the Inquisition did the rest. The post-war boom in consumer luxury in the USA collided with a better-late-than-never appreciation of rhythm and blues from the well-heeled white folk. Rock and roll was born, stolen, repackaged and flogged mercilessly to a world awash with radios and the nascent home owner-ship of televisions. It was soul music raised from the bitter sweat of oppression. A beguiling combination of sharecrop rhapsodies and devil-dealing blues riffs, merged with the freshly electrified instruments, souped up like a hot-rod engine. From that moment it became a universal language, absorbing all the musical dialects of the world into a glorious Esperanto, or – perhaps more accurately – a Tower of Babel with winklepickers. It became a self-perpetuating object, outside all control or understanding, even from its creators. It morphed, mutated and sprouted into ever more tantalising forms. Gyrating hips and lewd behaviour soundtracked by a righteous rhythm were beamed into the parlours of once-respectable neighbourhoods. For the old, it spelt the end of civilisation. For the young, it was time for action. The war had begun. The warriors of this conflict were beginning to reveal themselves to me. The food-dyed punk on his chopper. The long-haired dude on the bus to Slough with patched flares and a T-shirt emblazoned with

'In Search of Space'. The androgenous energy of that lonely figure with the eyeliner and Bowie bags whistling 'Heroes' as they stocked the shelves of Fisher and Sons supermarket. The check-out girl with short, bleached hair and a perpetual snarl. The sistren in the octagon centre with locks and Stepping Razor shirts. My brother.

In fact, two brothers: Jan and Ragnor. My brothers were an enigma to me. For starters, I could not work out why or how they were my brothers. Once during a minor disagreement about some trivial issue, I had threatened to tell my father of Jan's wrongdoing. 'I'm going to tell my dad on you,' I said. 'He's my dad too,' Jan replied. How was this possible? Jan and Ragnor did not live with us in our home in Rouge Mount Road. They were simply occasional visitors whose appearances I looked forward to very much, but surely not family. Families lived in the same home; wasn't that how it was supposed to be? They weren't even English. I mean, they spoke excellent English but with an unmistakable accent that my father had once confided to me was a Swedish twang. They were Swedes just like Abba. This meant they were excellent, but this hardly qualified them as brothers. Soon I would be able to report back to God that I had discovered betrayal.

My father was a rising star in telecoms or something. I wasn't really sure; all I knew was he was away most of the time on business trips and that meant duty free chocolate. In fact, he was away so often that for the first few years of my life I was sure he was merely a distant, taciturn chocolate-bearing relative, rather than my biological father. Guilt dripped from every Lindt selection box he delivered into our hands. My mother and I were left to fend for ourselves in the dangerous waters of metro land while he sealed deals in the back rooms of Nairobi nightclubs, Hong Kong Go-Go bars or Parisian parlours. The trinkets of tax-free shopping hung heavy with the scent of indiscretion. My mother would squirt the Opium pour femme and eye my father with suspicion. This suspicion was born from the nature of their meeting, a meeting that also explained the reason why my brothers were Swedish and were in fact my brothers. My parents had been neighbours. Neighbours in a reverse transnational coupling. My father was married to a Swedish woman, a neuroscientist by trade. My mother was married to Bjorn Borg's tennis coach. But dissatisfied, for some never explained reason – perhaps long, cold winters or perpetual summer daylight, who knows. Suffice it to say they coupled out of wedlock and, nine months later, as is the way with our species, Jonah Plantagenet was born. Bastard son of a Demon God. My parents returned to the United Kingdom with me in my swaddling clothes, leaving their families behind them. Two brothers. In fact, it was three brothers and a sister, but that is for another time. For now, we shall concern ourselves with only Jan and Ragnor. Ragnor was the oldest; dry, sharp, fiercely intelligent, with a dislike of space rock and a love of history. At an early age he had been subjected to a full three-hour Hawkwind gig without the aid of drugs and had been scarred for life by his experience. Ragnor was almost an adult when I first met him and thus somewhat out of my orbit of understanding. But Jan was hip. Jan wore denim. Jan had sneakers on his feet and an unorthodox haircut. On his visits he brought delicious sweets shaped like fish that knocked all British confectionary into a cocked hat. He also brought records. Every visit was a new opening, a new report to file to my divine patron. Jan would pull the sleeves from his Adidas sports bag. The covers came with fantastic images of other worlds or sweat-drenched warlocks getting down. These magicians were truly sons and daughters of demons. These were the awkward offspring of Santo whose riffs and rhymes, choruses and chords were attempts to find some way out of the prison our faulty consciousnesses had constructed. We opened the lid of my parents' wood-veneered radiogram and placed the record on the turntable. First it was Zeppelin, Black Sabbath and Rush; then PIL, The Fall and Jah Woosh. As the needle fell into the groove, I checked the threads and haircuts on the sleeves and compared them to the artists on the covers of my parents' meagre collection. They weren't even in the same galaxy. These cats weren't hip at all. They had bad matching crinoline suits and ruffled shirts in shades of colour that might have been developed by ICI's weapons division. Some looked like sex criminals. Others looked like recently liberated cult members before their deprogramming. Even Abba looked wanting in their matching white jumpsuits compared to DEVO or Kraftwerk. I began to realise that, although Abba had played their part, it was time to thank them and move on. Perhaps I would visit them again in a few years once my investigations were more advanced. The needle hit the groove, and everything changed. It was an insolent noise that demanded opposition to all forms of conventional living. Now the sounds that spat out of the radiogram's speakers were telling me to burn it all down, to make unholy alliances with the teenage hormones that were only a few months away from ripping my young body apart.

I'm digging fast now. The number of pills I've taken has passed half a dozen and is approaching double figures. The sirens are getting louder. It was only just over a decade ago that the Portuguese had given the Estado Novo the boot. I was sure elements sympathetic to the fascist junta still dwelt in the police force. They were coming for me now. An ambassador of a dangerous new youth craze. A drug cult of satanic dimensions. We brought love and hypnotic ritual music, but they saw only feckless junkies and tuneless repetition. Fuck! Dig, man, dig. The Nazi bully boys are coming. I pause while my friend passes me a beer and offers the cleft of their hand for a hoof of some undefined powder. Woosh. Dig, man, dig. The junta has risen. I'm down past the dinosaurs and into the Palaeozoic. Freaky arthropods and Silurian hepcats. This was the scene before T-Bone Walker plugged in. Before Lydon and all that new wave jazz. I'm sweating in my trench and the siren just gets louder. Dizzi is there digging in the sand with me. We are three years old, and we just mind-zapped one of our kindergarten classmates for info. Me and Diz met a few minutes ago and our bond is instant. In that moment we are everywhere at once: at a Cramps show, hunkered down over a mirror in a bedsit, in an Argentine hotel room, in a motel bathroom about to expire, riding bikes through Chaffinch-On-The-Hill, giving best man speeches, holding each other's wrinkled hands in a care home. The siren is getting louder. A new kid from out of town has rocked up in year one, saying he's from the US of A. The place where the rock and roll seed had germinated. Dizzi looks at me and we bury him in the sandpit. He doesn't struggle as Dizzi has zapped him good with hypno rays. Just his head and shoulders are poking out of the sand. I suck out the info from his brain with my vampire suckers and we leave him to come round.

'Lou, Lou, what have you done? Why are your pockets full of sand?' The teacher is pissed off. The kid is called Lou Reed. We become good friends and he's none the wiser, having no recollection of his entombment in the sandpit. But now Dizzi and I know about wide open highways, the Pilgrim Fathers, witch trials, land grabs, massacres, Custer's last stand, turkeys, pale face chicanery, theft, poison blankets, horror, slavery, civil war, civil rights, assassination, the Bay of Pigs, Vietnam, Levis, NYC, Max's Kansas City, CBGBS and brand-new Cadillacs.

It was 1980. Jan had come to visit with his sibling credentials now fully established. His hair was kind of long but not in a hippy way, side swept and unkempt. It felt like more of an anti-fashion statement. The denim had given way to thrift store chic. He had records. New records from the past. *White Light/White Heat*. It's just like Sister Ray said. This record comes from the deep Satanic pits of Santo's workshop. The factory. Deep underground, the Velvet Underground. One song is barely two minutes long and sounds like drugs, while another has a Welsh man discussing the US postal service and drilling into a lovelorn man's head over a languid fuzz and feedback trip that also sounds like drugs. 'Sister Ray' is seventeen minutes of controlled madness that sounds like the aftermath of drugs. I needed two showers and counselling after my first listen. Once I had recovered, I checked the cover of this remarkable, fuzz-laden gospel, expecting to see the name of my friend God on the line-up, but instead I saw the name of my old kindergarten comrade. Lou Reed. There he was again up to his neck in sand, handing out wisdom. I was ingesting the good, good nutrients with my vampire suckers.

I'm digging so fucking hard I think my fingers might snap. The cassette player is playing 'I.C. Love Affair' by DFC Team. It could be Pickering, Tonka Sound System,

Alfredo, Williams, Weatherall. It could be me. It's a cheesy number in some ways but makes total sense. The song contains a warning: *secret police is looking for me.*

The night before, we had put on an acid house party for a group of bewildered student graduates. They were dressed in gowns and mortar boards celebrating the end of years of hard study. They were hoping for some Michael Jackson and a slow dance at the end. We gave them a relentless barrage of acid trance, hip house and Italo piano-led canterers with a live PA by some heavily pilled-up, ex-squat kids from the grove on synths. They got Carly Simon's 'Why' at the end, which was a smoocher of sorts. Some got down and got it. You could see them change. It was a kind of magic. Others just drifted off into the night to find something more palatable. Some threw fruit fished from their cocktails. A lemon landed on 'The Chase' by Model 500; it skipped a bit, but I was too high to care.

The siren has stalled into a nagging whine, the thought police are coming armed with cocktail garnish and truncheons. Dizzi is in the pit with me. 'I met God in the forest,' I say. 'She gave me a mission to fulfil, a gnostic quest she called it,' I add, matter-of-factly, as I dig.

'Me too,' Dizzi replies. 'Not in the forest but on the train to High Wycombe. She was in the smoking carriage reading a copy of *2000AD*. How strange.'

He's grinning wildly as he too hammers into the sand with his hands. I guess we'll never know why we had been chosen. God said that, although all were called, few took up the challenge. As we sat in our sandpit with the head of Lou Reed poking up through the grit, we could see our school chums stretched out through time, playing with skipping ropes, singing rhymes that synchronised with the swing. We could see pencil cases and school bags with love hearts professing adoration for the latest pop combo or solo artiste. We could see carvings on desks. Punk's not dead. Glam's not dead. Folk rock's not dead. Synth pop's not dead. But by the time the kids turned into adults and the routine of life bit hard, it was all dead. But Dizzi and I, and perhaps a handful of other acolytes of righteous sound, continued to carry the weight of the curse. God's curious mission to find out why we shouldn't all be atomised by thunderbolts immediately. Music was the key that would unlock that mystery, even now I could feel it.

Before words there was sound. Before painting or pictogram there was noise. A baby is born screaming into the world, singing its first shrill notes. Like the chick, the foal, the calf. The mantle cracks and booms as the lava hisses. The Earth born into sound. Everywhere there is rhythm and music. Something about that pulse transcends the concerns of the eternal, pitiless human will and plugs you into the hum of the void. Beyond representation or object. It was release, but it was also a profound fusion with eternity and a clue as to what made the universe tick. Record and radio were the transmitters of the void's holy message. This I knew. Now God knew too. Three years old with my vampire suckers deployed into the brain of a proto-punk rock hero.

'I saw Lou on the cover of a record the other day. You remember Lou? Nice lad, quiet with lovely hair.' I feel quite chatty as the rhythm of our digging synchronises.

'Good old Lou. He had such a delicious mind. I shan't forget him in a hurry,' Dizzi replies as we hit the late 1980s.

'I wonder what Lou makes of acid house?' I ask as the siren stops. There's a policeman inside my head and he must be destroyed.

Mixtape to Placate the Fascist Bully Boy Portuguese Police Force in My Sand Bunker

Side One

1. *Mysteries of the East – Jhalib*
2. *Spicy – G-Force*
3. *Etno Techno – 4T Thieves*
4. *Ska East – United Eye*
5. *Baba Mhmmm – Bee Buzz*
6. *Keep on Giving (Justin Robertson Remix) – Dub Federation*
7. *Maracaibo – La Unión*
8. *Relax Your Soul – Fun 4 Fun*
9. *Jazzy John's Freestyle Dub – StoneBridge*
10. *Whole Lotta Love – Massimo Barsotti*

11. *Taboo – Hypnotique*

12. *I'll Be Waiting (Red Zone Mix) – Clive Griffin*

13. *Corazon De Rubi – Los Chunguitos*

Side Two

1. *Funk Express – UF Force*

2. *Problèms D'Amour – Alexander Robotnick*

3. *Out'A the Box – Jiraffe*

4. *Ring of Fire – Bang a Gong*

5. *Shogunade – Ryuchi Sakamoto*

6. *Ou Est Le Soleil – Paul McCartney*

7. *Vital Rise – Sidecut>DB*

8. *I'm Starving – Vanilla Sound Corps*

9. *Apocalypse – Voltage Control*

10. *Greater Reward – Severed Heads*

11. *Pump & Whine – Major Maestro*

12. *Hills of Katmandu – Tantra*

13. *They Came in Peace – Tranquillity Bass*

7

Newsagents

There are many ways a confession can be delivered. In front of a jury. Twelve randomly selected members of the public throwing up into handkerchiefs as the testimony is read out. Under torture, sputtering out details of your crimes whilst being waterboarded by some government thug. Death bed confessions are popular. As the shadows close in and all the hard-won accolades of a lifetime suddenly seem completely pointless. When the cold fear grips and you begin to wonder: is there a hell and am I about to find myself in it? That's when the urge to clear the conscience takes you. But the lengthening shadows are but portents of the great release of nothingness. The emptiness – that is, the ground of all being – cares little for sin. As for hell, yeah, sure there's a hell. But it isn't a geographical location or a spiritual state, it's the doom of being reborn. One might confess to a priest. This is a neat way of doing it because, take it from me, God is not one for harsh judgments. She is simply curious and, seeing as heaven is nothing like they say in the brochures, anything you are required to do by way of penance is largely pointless. I'm delivering mine via this book, which is also a cool way to do it because, as I stated at the beginning (or was it the end?), I am dead. So, I won't have to read all the crummy reviews or reappraisals of my life and work by whatever generation of new puritans get to decide such things in the future. In my time we had the internet and social media. This probably seems ridiculous to you now, as archaic as a Socratic symposium, but in my day we took to various online platforms to reveal our inner-most secrets. However, these were largely fictions designed to make the poster seem more interesting than they actually were. I include myself in that tawdry pantomime.

In my life I was seldom honest. God's gifts included a poker face, a knack for spinning convincing yarns and a literally God-given talent for styling it out when faced by embarrass-ing gaps in my knowledge. It started by lying to my mother about stains on the bedspread and ended with denying my part in the ritual sacrifice of an unfortunate backpacker. I would lie about all sorts of things in order to complete my mission from God. It was necessary if I was to ingratiate myself with the cognoscenti. Have you read? Oh yes, of course. Do you know the work of the Venezuelan abstract expressionist? Why yes, I have one of their lithographs in my studio. Do you know the first album by…? I have it on vinyl. What was you first gig? Silver Apples jamming with Suicide with Robbie Shakespeare on bass, The Monks were the support act, and I think Sherwood was doing the sound? It was at a wee birthday bash for Fontella Bass hosted by Richard Brautigan. Truly it was Rush at Wembley Arena, not that there's anything wrong with that. But now that I'm dead I don't feel the urge to fabricate my history anymore. What was the first record you bought? Elvis Coste— Nah. Fuck it. It was 'Hot From the Lock' by Flintlock.

God bestowed many gifts on me to help me on my way; however, liquid childhood financial arrangements were not one of them. I was young and hungry for fresh kicks but cash poor. I still loved sweets and comics, but since the coming of Abba and my subsequent baptism into rock and roll, records would have to be accommodated within my meagre budget. Choices would have to be made. God did not offer easy lines of credit. What God offered were portals and fetishes, keys for unlocking mysteries. Keys to the vaults where records lived. Nothing is ever straightforward in any gnostic quest and these portals were often tricky to find. Some would hide in plain sight and sometimes turn out to be locations you'd visited on many occasions but had not previously appreciated their magical qualities. Such was it with the NSS newsagents in Chaffinch- On-The-Hill's brutalist shopping arcade. More accurately Chaffinch-Under-The-Hill, the ancient name for this particular location before the hill folk descended and annexed the land from the people of the valley. Now everything was Chaffinch-On-The-Hill, even the low-lying shopping arcade. The arcade was a perplexing carbuncle nestling at the foot of a slope the locals called the Silver Mound. Silver Mound was either a former burial site of a renowned bronze age chieftain or the slag heap formed when the railway cutting was dug out. It was unclear as to whether this was the hill referred to in 'On-The-Hill' or just another incline in this gently undulating part of the world. It was everything you'd expect from a metro land ribbon development with mock Tudor shop fronts housing charity shops and estate agents. A church-run gift shop selling weird tat that you'd never dream of gifting anyone. A coffee shop with a fine selection of home baked cakes. (A coffee shop that was in fact a portal, but more of that later.) But the shopping centre at the foot of the hill shared none of this mildly offensive conservativism. It was radically hideous. A monument to a civilisation in terminal decline with no more ideas left to save it from barbarism. It lacked any aesthetic finesse, comprising as it did a car park surrounded by a covered concrete walkway under which a bland array of corporate outlets squatted unenthusiastically. A shoe shop selling footwear even a gulag inmate would turn their nose up at. An optician whose inventory was imported from Orwell's Airstrip One. A frozen food shop with more E numbers in its food than an orbital rave. A newsagent. NSS. The first portal of many.

Time travel is hard and requires sacrifice. Usually, this amounts to simple self-mutilation, and only rarely does it require more outré offerings. I sliced a gash into my skin and let the blood ooze out. The unwilling plasma bubbled and fell onto the makeshift time altar that I had constructed from ready-at-hand household objects.

Items required for makeshift time machine[*]

1. *Table lamp (preferably with a curly flex and faulty wiring)*
2. *Tin box full of nails*
3. *Wire from a mattress spring. (Mattress must be sourced from a fly-tipping location and have stains on it suggestive of unsavoury activity)*
4. *Hand-driven drill*
5. *A cassette compilation of current pop hits rendered by a barely competent combo of session musicians*
6. *Uncooked rice*
7. *The flag of any former imperial power's merchant navy*

As the blood hit the altar a vortex began to form. Down the time tunnel I could see a million possible futures spi-

---

[*] All or none of these items are essential. Human blood must be spilt for any or none of these components to function in the desired manner. Failure to follow instructions will lead to temporal fracture and certain rebirth. The cycle continues.

ralling in all directions. Then the vortex had me. My spilt blood cells carrying my encoded self into the teeming temporal lanes. I was sucked in, spun around and spat out into the time before records. An ancient locus. This was a time with a different kind of magic. Music was a fleeting performance existing only in the now. My blood congealed and solidified; it sprouted arms, legs and ears. I wandered about in the time before records. First I heard a crackle like the hiss of scratched vinyl. It was the molten ball forming the mantle. Boom, crash, crack, crack again. Mountains rise. The soft sound of water falling onto thirsty ground from newly hatched clouds. Oceans form. I wander on across continents. Still no sign of God; this is strictly an amateur enthusiasts' operation. Soon there is song. Algae song. Mushroom song. Plant song. It's good stuff. Catchy in an atonal modal jazz kind of way. Then come single cell creatures who go in for a drone-like throb. Soon they're crawling on land and it's a whole fucking symphony. There is sound. Before anyone heard it there was sound. Before anyone wrote down a single clef or crochet there was sound. In fact, I had been hanging out for literally billions of years in the time before records before I heard anything like the screech of humanity.

I was relaxing with a troop of orangutans who were trying out a new number they'd been working on. It had a nice beat. I could feel the influence of mid-six million years BC surf punk in its rhythm. The lyrics weren't great, all about mating and eating fruit, but they worked with the music, so I was into it. Jacky, the drummer, told me their cousins were dropping by for a jam later and asked if I'd like to stick around. Sure thing, I said, I have no prior engagements. Come dusk the cousins arrived. A small tribe of Homo Sapiens and some Neanderthal dudes. We shook hands. The human types broke out the booze, the orangutans had some edibles which we shared, then we got into it. Such great music we made. Primates getting down with fermented hooch and psychedelics – fucking perfect. The humans had some tight tunes and good moves. They were hopping and jiving, shuffling and running on the spot like demons. The Miocene epoch was jumping. We all clapped along and got down with them. The older ape musicians took notes, the humans had some nice riffs. Their singing was intriguing too, starting as it did as a parody of animal grunts or birdsong, but soon finding its own distinct form. It was ugly but effective. The orangutans were digging it heavily. Human lyrics were cool too. Songs about mating and motorcars. The party went on until sunrise but ended in an unfortunate fracas when a fucked-up human let the liquor get the better of them, spilling drinks, getting into a fight with the ape pack's beta male, before finally running off with the remaining mushroom tincture. The rest of the human cousins then followed suite, turning on the older apes and each other before disappearing into the jungle with the booze. The orangutans headed back into the treetops and vowed not to invite those arseholes again even if they did have great record collections.

> *'Why do people make art? Evolution and survival of the fittest? And yet humans are spectacularly ill-equipped for survival. Why aren't we molluscs?'*
> Alfred North Whitehead

Mollusc art is spectacular. But I wasn't born a mollusc so I can't speak for its intention. I am, however, a son of a demon God, so I'll restrict my observations to what I know. I followed the human tribe back into the forest hoping to feed on their awakening consciousness. They weren't a bad bunch, just a bit unsophisticated. They were like awkward youngsters copying their older siblings, much like myself. Vague approximations just short of the mark. Unable to grow fur or feathers of their own, they hacked off the pelts of other animals and draped them awkwardly over their own inadequate bodies. Graceless runners, sloppy swimmers, unable to take flight without the help of machinery. They mimicked the noises of nature too. This started as an unpleasant guttural groan, but soon they found their own music. A distillation of their fracturing from the world and their attempts to reconnect with it. Songs of love, songs of loss, songs of praise for a God who knew nothing of their existence. This was what I had come to find. I sucked deep from the marrow of the fledgling species. My vampire suckers drew the blood from their veins and the notes from their souls. If it wasn't for the unstoppable tide of experience that replenished all that I had taken, they would have been mere husks once I had finished with them. I was bloated and full. I hoped God would be pleased.

I was glad I had packed my Clark's desert treks, their pasty-like construction perfect for comfortable time travel where the loafer or even the brogue can be too rigid for prolonged temporal wanderings. From the cave dwelling shaman conducting fireside rites, tribes dancing around the flames, bonding with the shadows, bonding with each other, to the first wandering minstrel, the first music pro, the first rock and roll star. Music evolved even as we evolved. Growing more intricate, codified into written notation with symbols representing complex syncopation and mul-tilayered instrumentation before being stripped back to its rhythmical basics again and again. Harp, sistrum, lute and lyre. Three chords now form a band. Evolution is not progress, it's just a change of direction, like a DJ reading the room. Musical fluidity is eternal. Music is beyond mere packaging, production or reproduction. It is beyond performance, criticism, notation, sign or signifier. Once made or played it becomes something indescribably won-derful or puzzlingly terrible. We can never tell or predict the outcome. Music is a weapon. Music is the sword that cuts the veil. Music is a tool. The telescope that sees every-thing at once. Music is a city. The place where all thought dies and reveals itself as pure feeling. Music is no- thing. Like God. That's why God turned me on to it. She knew that's where knowledge of the human soul would lie. In the disagreement of the organism with its own equations. Because music is the greatest challenge to all our attempts to quantify of our world. Music is number. Music is beyond counting. It speaks a different language to science or poetry. It can be analysed, monitored, dissected, disembowelled, given ranks, likes, customer reviews, column inches; it has been translated into graphs, sine waveforms, diagrams and scores. But these are just exercises in formalisation and containment, so none of them come close to understanding or describing its essence. Because music has no essence. It just is. Even when constrained by notation and recording, its essence escapes capture. The score was the first attempt to imprison the transitory magical moment and commodify it. Early capitalism ruining the fun as usual. Then came wax cylinders, records, CDs, mp3s, wavs and digital streams. They did much better at ensnaring a moment in time and freezing it. Like the written word, it was a story made into an artefact. The magic made object. A fetish. A product whose creation and dissemination those in authority hoped to control and profit from. It was a trap. A snare to catch the wild sound and put it on display. But it was also an unexpected gateway. Like all good objects, scores and records took on new meanings and functions from those intended by 'the man'. They became messengers whose message was music, but whose substance broke free from the designs of their maker and became fucking living entities. I was staring at one of them now.

On my return from the time before records I decided to take out my brand new three-speed racer and put it through its paces by riding fast down Silver Mound. It was Saturday. I had pocket money, the knowledge gleaned from time travel and brother Jan's sports holdall. I needed records if I was to become an effective teenager. But funds were not plentiful and even paper rounds don't pay what they used to. There were inflationary pressures. My bicycle was red. The colour of war, anger, love and religious fervour. A red Raleigh. I'd hoped for a ten-speed or at worst a five, but a three-speed? Why the fuck had my mother picked out a three-speed? Did she want me to suffer? After meditating on it for a time I realised that this was just another lesson in disappointment, and that once I had accepted the limitations of three-geared travel, I would find the road just as long and with as many potholes as any ten-geared rider. It was all about surrendering to the now. I didn't need ten gears or five, I just needed to try harder. Besides, some bikes didn't have any gears, so I should count myself lucky. I grew to love my red, three-geared disappointment engine and rode it enthusiastically along the lanes. The shop fronts flew by in a blur. Familiar business signs were stretched to become temporary echoes. I travelled across borders. Down the Silver Mound and into the Chaffinch-On-The-Hill shopping centre. The wind whistled in my ears as I descended. In the wind there was a whisper. The soothing voice of God. Open the door, step inside. Open the door, step inside.

The red baron skidded to a halt. The red baron was the name I had just given my three-speed bicycle. Good name, I thought. Edgy. I was outside the door of NSS newsagents. I'd been there a hundred times before. For papers and sweets, magazines and comics. My father's eyes wandering to the top shelf, my eyes following his. But today the door looked different. I don't recall ever seeing the mysterious mist, the seraphim blowing trumpets or the garlands of live serpents twisting around the door frame before, nor was I familiar with the unearthly glow emanating from the racks just beyond the A to Zs. The whisper of God's voice came again through the mist. Open the door step inside. Open the door step inside. Thanks to the functioning of the modern proximity detector, entry was easy. I just strode up and stepped in. Inside things were, on the surface at least, quite normal. People were flicking through magazines. Some openly. Some more furtive. Kids were scoping ice cream. Tots were screaming. Teens were buying cigs. But there was also change, something suggestive of a great transformation hanging in the air.

NSS carried cassettes for car stereos. Eight tracks. Ferric. Chrome. Metal. NSS carried records. It was no HMV, but it did its best to serve the community in its quest for pop thrills. I approached the racks. I pulled out sleeves. Some

I recognised from my neighbours' wire metal record racks. Easy listening LPs populated by familiar sex criminals in crinoline. Uneasy looking girls in swimsuits, crop tops or hot pants with lists of charts hits covered by low-paid session musicians. Pastoral scenes containing popular classical numbers interpreted by low-rent orchestras. Music for pleasure. But dotted here and there were other faces. Women. Men. Hybrid non-conforming entities. Alien creatures. Demon Gods. Nestling uncomfortably next to less threatening monsters. I pulled them out and studied them all. But inexperience was hampering my investigations. They all had hair of varying anti-establishment lengths, denim, guitars etc. How could one tell the chancers from the revolutionaries? Inexperience, but also hunger, was gnawing at my confidence like a ghoul. I was a young boy, still at least partially human, and human children need sweets. Curly Wurlys didn't come cheap and penny chews were deceptively priced as one or even two was never enough. I loved sweets and could be confident of their provenance, but records were a mystery. Records were expensive too, especially the ones with the most countercultural characters on the sleeves. A balance must be found. My fingers flicked and fidgeted; I was aware of the shopkeeper eyeing me suspiciously. I must decide. Panic overtook me. I decided that, like Rhinehart's Dice Man, I would let chance decide. I closed my eyes and thrust out my hand blindly into the rack marked 'sale', trusting fate would provide me with something worthy from the bargain bucket end of the market. My fingers seemed to stretch out to impossible lengths. Choirs of satyrs sang as they danced around the fires of my childhood. Through the smoke an image of unstoppable youth rebellion took shape in my hands. Flintlock 'Hot From the Lock' emerged from the racks like Excalibur from the lake. 99p.

The portal closed and I was back in the unfussy interior of NSS newsagents. I studied the artefact. They kind of looked the part. Long hair. Electric instruments. Good price too. I took my prize to the counter, paid and left with a pocket full of chews – and the Curly Wurly too.

8

Denim: God Fabric

'We were rebelling against the establishment, for Chrissake.
You go fight a goddamn war, and the minute you get back
and take of the uniform and put on Levis and leather jackets,
they call you an asshole.'
Wino Willie Forkner

I will rejoice greatly in the Lord,
My soul will exult in my God.
For She has clothed me with garments of salvation,
She has wrapped me with a robe of righteousness,
God, *Isaiah 61:10*

A clerk of the court walks up and down in front of the jury as the crowd in the public gallery hoots and hollers. The clerk is wearing a piece of evidence that has been entered into the record as prosecution exhibit 23. The clerk wrinkles his nose and tries to remain professional as the catcalls from the gallery get louder. The judge repeatedly bangs the gavel in a vain attempt of regaining control of the proceedings. The item of evidence causing so much commotion is a denim jacket with its sleeves cut off. It smells of engine grease and patchouli oil. There is crusted blood around a ragged hole that looks to have been caused by a knife or sword. The jury recoils from the reeking rag as the clerk models the prosecution's exhibit so that all can take in the details of the item. On the back of the jacket are a set of patches arranged in a stinking oval. Between the top rocker and the bottom rocker there is an insignia that, under the grime, looks like two spoons crossed under a slice of cake. The patches surrounding the insignia read: Naughty Boys Motorcycle Club.

'Members of the jury, I beg your indulgence once again,' the lead prosecutor begins. He pauses and trains his gaze on the jury. Then, like a magnet herding iron filings, he pulls the jury's eyes with his own to rest on the bloody, cut-off denim jacket. His words flow with a profoundly morbid poetry. 'The continuous litany of horrible crimes you have had to endure would test the stoutest heart. Yet I must now put before you further horrors. Horrors that can barely be described by word or picture. Not only will this chapter reveal the wicked acts of theft, deception and murder that the accused so happily indulges himself in, but it will also shine a light on yet another heinous act of perversion and criminality that will shock you to your very core. That crime is the crime against fashion.'

Gasps from the jury. The prosecutor continues.

'Crimes against fashion so despicable that I trust the learned judge will not fail to pass the harshest sentence available to this court on the fiend sat right there in front of you all! There must be no mercy shown to this boy. For the abuses of hat, coat and trouser he so gleefully committed, he must pay the ultimate price when the inevitable guilty verdict is reached.'

The prosecutor's voice rises in pitch and volume as he points his long, shaky finger at young Jonah Plantagenet, who is grinning from the witness box. There are further gasps and an awkward silence. The judge looks mystified and asks a question of the defence.

'Is it not somewhat presumptuous of the prosecution to predetermine the outcome and probable sentence resulting from this trial? Does the defence not wish to object?'

'Not at all, my lud. The prosecution is entirely correct; my client is clearly guilty,' replies the defence council.

✕

Wino Willie rode into Hollister at the head of the Booze-fighters MC on the 4th of July 1947. I was there riding pillion with my long hair spilling out behind me like demon wings. On my legs I wore Levis encrusted with spilt beer and the dust of the road. I had recently been demobbed from the US marine corps. Two tours island hopping in the Pacific, then a stint with the occupying forces in Japan under General Douglas MacArthur before I was cashiered out for selling bootleg whiskey and ammunition to the Yakuza. Back in early 1980s Chaffinch-On-The-Hill, I had sliced a few layers of skin from my thumb and placed them into the interface of my makeshift time machine. My intention was to gather data on conflict clothing as I had recently acquired a Vietnam War era US Army M65 combat jacket, which I had customised with a crude copy of the artwork from Gong's 'Live Floating Anarchy' and was thus interested in the semiotics of military garments adopted by utopian youth movements. My skin cells travelled down the time lanes, splitting off into various eras of conflict that I felt combined brutality with a certain sartorial panache.

There is one strange aspect of time travel that is occasionally touched on in the literature: it's very draughty. People often talk about the winds of time, but few ever experience its biting chill. In my early years I was blessed with long flowing locks, which gradually morphed into a flat top, then a crew cut, a skinhead and, finally, the patchy mosaic of male pattern baldness. This inevitable failure of my hair follicles led me to favour hats as a means of keeping the draught of time at bay until I could rob the scalp of someone whose haircut I desired. I set out through the time lanes in search of cool hats. My first stop was the fourth century BC. My family never really went on holiday; we had spent some time in Hayling Island and once rented a cottage in Norfolk, but the rest of the world was a mystery to all of us except my father, who had visited pretty much every corner of the globe, as he was fond of reminding us on the few occasions he was at home long enough *to* remind us. So, with my newfound God-given gifts I decided I would not only travel through time but also through space. It was thus that I arrived in fourth century BC Anatolia, home of the Phrygian people. This particular time and place was blessed with its fair share of vicious inter-clan conflict and a new line in head gear modelled on the cap favoured by one of the region's gods. The Phrygian cap. I was on speaking terms with the god in question. His name was Attis. The designated god of vegetation. Attis was at the time thinking of castrating himself in an act of ceremonial magic. He often called me worried that this might be a rash decision. He thought perhaps his actions could be viewed as being a little extreme and, knowing that I was on good terms with God, wondered if I might offer him some friendly advice on whether or not he should proceed with the operation. I told him that I was not yet thirteen years old and so poorly equipped with wisdom. However, it struck me that, as a vegetation deity, what Attis was really involved in was a symbolic act of pruning. His parts would grow again as surely as a privet hedge in spring. Attis seemed reassured by my advice and said he would most likely proceed as the local population were hoping for a good harvest and were urging genital pruning as the most likely guarantee of success. He urged me to visit at my earliest convenience. It was a Wednesday when I knocked on the deity's door. His wife Cybele, great mother of gods, answered the door with tear-stained eyes. This was not a reassuring sight. Cybele proceeded to explain that Attis had carried out his planned self-castration and was now dead. Thankfully he had neglected to tell Cybele of my previous encouragement, and so I was warmly welcomed into the temple like a long-lost son. Thanking me for my steadfast friendship, Cybele handed me a parcel. It was a gift from Attis bequeathed to me with his last breath as he writhed in his death throes on the temple floor. It was a cap. A conical felt number that bent slightly at its apex. A Phrygian cap. I checked my reflection in the surface of some polished goblets. It looked fabulous. I adjusted it to a jaunty angle, thanked the great mother of gods and went on my way. However, as it turned out, my previous prediction was correct, for not long after I had disappeared back down the time lanes, Attis was resurrected and reborn like a flower in springtime, and he wanted his hat back. Fuck that, it looked mega on me – I'm keeping it.

Conscious of the angry vegetable god's pursuit, I enacted a few swift manoeuvrers through time, seeding the Phrygian cap into multiple scenarios as I went, hoping to throw Attis off the scent. In Rome it became the symbol of emancipated slaves. On the Delaware, as Washington paddled silently, it was on the heads of the tax dodging revolutionary army. In France, as the Bastille burned and the guillotine was oiled, the 'sans-culottes' wore the bonnet rouge as a symbol of liberty. All the while I wore the box-fresh original on my youthful scalp. I adapted it as a watch cap as I travelled the frozen sea on convoy duty to Murmansk. U-boats stalked the ships while the Junkers bombers dived and harried the decks. The fabric was now wool, slick with sweat and soot. In the twenty-first century it became the headwear of choice for hipster youth trying to look rugged as they sipped oat milk lattes in hot desk office buildings. Attis, all the while, sought me out. But what, dear reader, am I guilty of here? Not theft, surely; it was a gift given in good faith by a castrated god. I refuse to feel guilty about it. I was generous. I gave the Phrygian cap to the world. See how cool it looks. Just check out Jacques Cousteau. You should be thanking me, not prosecuting me.

It's 3rd July 1969. I am one year old. I'm lying face down in a laurel bush wearing striped loon pants, a crushed velvet jacket and Attis's Phrygian cap. My Chelsea boots are sticking out of the hedge, wiggling from side to side in time to a song inside my head. It's a nagging, beautiful chant. Pharoah Sanders. *The Creator Has a Masterplan.* The hypnotic chant is rising and falling in my bombed-out skull. The saxophone charging insolently through the scales. Shakers shaking. The whole damn combo tuning into the void. God is lying next to me, and she is totally tripping out.

'This is it, Jonah! This is fucking it! It almost makes me believe I do have a masterplan! Lord knows I wish I did.'

God rolls over and tries to take off my Phrygian cap, but she can't focus and pulls my nose instead. We both roll about laughing. This is holy music. So holy, in fact, that it's turning God into a believer. God flops over onto her back and stares up at the star-speckled sky. It's nearly midnight and we are in a Sussex Garden on the best acid God can provide. There is a relatively modest country pile belonging to a rock and roll star. He is having a party. He is always having parties. I've been here for years. The voice, saxophone, shakers and drums entwine in a terrifying crescendo of freeform madness. Every musical rule is twisted and spat out in a glorious explosion of love. God levitates off the ground, impossibly high.

'OH SHIT! OH SHIT!' God is shouting loudly. The saxophone emerges from the maelstrom and the band take off again. 'YES, JONAH, THIS IS THE SHIT!' God's voice shakes the foundations of the Earth as Pharoah blows. The same eight notes rotate and revolve, swirl and launch off into the wide-open sky. This is a prayer, but God has answered with a question. 'Tell me, Jonah, what can you see?' she asks, suddenly calm, lying still in the soft leaves of the laurel bush.

'Nothing,' I say.

'Good, good, that's my boy.' She takes my hand gently and we rise from the hedge. Far away the party is in full swing. Freak beat tones rattle off the old-fashioned windows. God is in the garden.

I try to focus my fractured eyes, but the acid is confusing the up with the down. Once my senses align, I see that I'm standing on a well-tended lawn. God has gone. She's always doing that, ducking out of the party just when it's getting interesting. I'm aware of the rippling of water and a blueish rectangle moving. Vibrating. A guy I met at the party is walking off back to the house. He is soaked, his cords make a sucking sound as he weaves across the lawn. He's out of it. Drunk by the looks of him. That familiar, purposeless stagger. I think I might head in. But what about a swim? Fuck, yes! Water on skin, that is what I need. I wish God was still here; she'd really dig swimming. I carelessly discard my loon pants on the lawn and, swirling my velvet jacket around my head like a helicopter, I run across the grass, over the cool grey paving and jump into the pool. Zing. The sensation is incredible. All my senses explode with an overwhelming feeling of oneness. I'm an amoeba at the dawn of time. A protozoon with a Phrygian cap on.

In sea. Water is dissolving and water is removing.
Taking me to the bottom of the ocean.

I'm in the sandpit with Dizzi. More heads are in the sand now. Mesmerised with our vampire suckers in their somnolent minds. David Byrne, the new boy, is in the pit. Sanders, Coltrane, Davis, Ayler, Dolphy, the whole Art Ensemble of Chicago. Smiling faces encased in the sand of our laboratory. I can hardly move, I'm so full. I surface in the pool and blow out a jet of water like a blue whale. I scream. I think that I'm alone, and that no one cares. But I'm not alone. I flap my arms, realising I'm only one year old and have not yet got the hang of swimming. But I'm a time traveller, so it quickly comes back to me. My thrashing arms take on a more regular rhythm. Doggy paddle slowly morphing into breaststroke. In the darkness I hit an obstacle. It's a body. Still. Face down in the water. I act as fast as any moral agent can and drag the body across the water, up the steps and out of the pool. I drop the body onto the paving stones. It's him. The rock and roll star. Fuck. What happened? Did I land on him in the dark as I jumped into the water? Had he passed out, too high to swim, too stoned to paddle? Was he pushed and held down? It was impossible to tell. I try to revive him with all the skills I have at my disposal. Mouth to mouth. Pressure. Heart pumping. Ritual chanting. Blood sacrifice. But he just won't come round. I hear a commotion from the house. The strains of 'The Young Mods' Forgotten

Story' skips across the lawn as a group of revellers burst out of the French windows laughing and screaming with joy, running towards the pool. For fun. For the celebration of life. They will be here any second. I look at the beautiful boy lying there by the pool. He looks like a fucking angel. His hair golden and sumptuous. Cut into a perfect bowl. I deploy my vampire suckers and assume his hairstyle before disappearing back into the time vortex.

The rock and roll star's haircut sat nicely under Attis's Phrygian cap. Occasionally I would take the cap off and let the wind whip my stolen locks. This was the first of many scalpings I would undertake. Not all my victims were dead either. In fact, most were very much alive and breathing when I took their hair. No one complained. Most were thankfully unaware of my crimes. I stole Bowie's hair on many occasions while he was still with us. The Berlin wave and the duke's slicked back elegance. 1976. Dave Brock and Robert Calvert are taking a stroll in the emerging plot of Meanwhile Gardens in the shadow of Erno Goldfinger's Trellick Tower. Local people are transforming the waste ground into something beautiful. Bob and Dave are discussing Quark, Strangeness and Charm and Alfred Jarry's pataphysical theories. Bob is pushing a bicycle. I'm dressed as a citizen of the mid-1970s and blend in perfectly with the local population. I'm tilling the soil. As they pass, deep in metaphysical conversation, I bang them both on the head with my hoe, knocking them out. While they are unconscious I steal

Dave's long hair and Bob Calvert's leather World War One flying hat. I later discard them both in a skip on the Latimer Road after trying to swap them for cheap speed, a 7-inch by the Swell Maps and a Baudrillard book I didn't understand, only to pluck them straight out again, because fuck it, they still sounded like the future. In my time, whatever that is, I've stolen Steve Marriot's French crew cut, Winston Rodney's locks, X Moore's MA1, Rob Tyner's bulbous dome, Joey Ramone's Converse, the beard of Thelonious Monk, Jimmy Cliff's strides, Weller's overcoat, sunglasses and loafers, Ornette Coleman's kufi hat, The Monk's robes, Lemmy's bullet belt, Thunderstick's mask, Bolan's curls (Bob Plant's too), Biff Byford's spandex tights, the Psychic TV, King Tubby's vest and Ryuichi Sakamoto's floppy fringe. All obtained using similar methods of criminal subterfuge. I would kindly ask the court of public opinion to consider at least ten thousand further counts of theft, too numerous to list in detail here (please refer to the index in the court files and charge sheet for details).

Geographical relocation is fun. I've always had a great time in the USA. It's the perfect spot for fiends like myself. Its culture is a mixture of optimism, invention and personal freedom awkwardly blended with genocidal violence, corruption, greed and naked prejudice, making it a microcosm of the whole human project. I don't mean to single out that great nation as the focus of criticism; every continent and time period has a similar trajectory of hope, despair and violence. But the USA gave us blue jeans and the Ricken-backer guitar, so I spent a lot of time gathering information for God from sea to shining sea. I'd first arrived on that continent with a bunch of dour cats called the Pilgrim Fathers. I stowed away on the Mayflower, initially attracted by the utilitarian cut of their tunics and the stout brims of their black, broad-brimmed hats. But as it turned out, they were a tiresome tribe of bigots, always burning each other for witchcraft, swindling the locals whose land they were in the process of stealing, or eating each other when stores ran low. But the worst thing about them was their taste in music. I thought with those big hats they wore it would be all Richie Blackmore guitar riffs or some Incredible String Band trippy madrigals. But it was nothing of the kind. Sure, they did some singing on holy days, but their songs were just psalms set to dirge-like lute riffs, which can be cool if you're Sunn O))), but in the hands of this lot it just lacked any conviction. The clubs were awful too. The Vikings at least had a few killer numbers, and their festival scene was rightly celebrated, but these invaders just weren't doing it for me. I hooked up with the Wampanoag people for a time before making my way across country to hang with the Cheyenne. These were bittersweet years that even this confession is not equipped to describe, so I'll leave that to those qualified to speak. I saw Custer going down at the Big Horn and wore his cursed moustache for a time until the stink got too much to bear. Now the Pilgrim Fathers had been joined by a whole bunch of adventurers from around the globe, and for better or worse they had made their way to the shores of the Pacific Ocean. Some of these cats were refugees from poverty, oppression and the intolerance of the Old World. Some were unscrupulous cut-throats. But fiends tend not to differentiate, so I joined up with a few different gangs of desperadoes. They had better tunes now. I could hear the unchained spirit of Africa, the Irish heart, Scandinavian laments, the passion of Mexico and the chug, chug, chug of the great iron horse. Songs of the road. Songs of the great, wide-open plains. Songs from the peaks and deep, deep valleys. Songs of hard times, chain gangs, betrayal and murder. Songs of death. I don't know if it was progress, but it was something new. Ballads born of blood that would in a few scant generations change the world. I had killer boots and a six-gun made of polished silver. A fair few notches on my belt, too. Jonah 'The Kid' Plantagenet, the fastest gun in Chaffinch-On -The-Hill. Men feared my name and coveted my dusty Phrygian cap. I drifted through time with blood on my hands.

I ended up in the mines just north of Frisco. We were digging for gold, or maybe diamonds or coal. We were always digging for something. The worms and the flies watched on in bemusement as we eked out a living extracting the shiny ore valued for its rarity and glistening qualities, at the behest of some other guys who lived above ground, high on the hog. As if there wasn't enough golden light available for free for at least half the day. One day, maybe even sunlight will be a currency. Humans' value rarity. I put that in my latest letter to God. Limited edition gatefold sleeve vinyl only. One day, as I was coming out of the mineshaft at the end of my shift, I bumped into God; she was shooting the breeze with some new faces who'd just bowled into town. They were looking for work. She looked much younger than she had in the woods of Chaffinch-On-The-Hill. Her hair was no longer silver-grey but instead a lustrous deep dark black. She was as beautiful as ever but slightly less wrinkly. She was dressed like a regular at the Taboo club. Light blue face paint with even brighter red lipstick thickly applied to form an exaggerated mouth. She had a tall, bright green Stetson on her head, also of fantastically exaggerated proportions. A red-and-white candy-striped silk blouse that looked like a parody of the stars and stripes, a high-waisted floor-length kilt in the MacDonald tartan and a pair of five-inch-high white patent stacked heel boots. I waved hello as I removed my Phrygian cap to mop my dirty, sweaty brow. She checked me out head to toe with her hand on her hip, striking a sassy pose.

'Hey, Jonah, looking good! What are those pants you got on? They are niiiice.'

I looked down at the filthy trousers I was wearing. I had picked them up at Heinemann's general store a couple of months ago. They *were* niiiice. Levi Strauss and Company, wide leg, cinch back, white selvedge from the Amoskeag denim factory, rivetted, single pocket, union-made blue fucking jeans, baby.

'Thanks, God,' I replied. 'They're practical for the job in hand, real comfy in the mine, or if I have a fancy taking a ride out across the plains on my horse, but I've a mind to adapt them as the uniform of a confident new youth movement in the middle to late twentieth century.'

'That's a great idea, Jonah. You might need to take them in a bit for those new wave kids,' God replied.

That's exactly what I did. God is full of great ideas when it comes to style. I did it all: bootcut, bell bottom, skinny, balloon cut, high-waisted, low rise, snow washed, stone wash, distressed, sanforised, shrink to fit, wide leg, straight leg, tapered, cut-off, rolled up, buckle back, zip fly, button fly, every permutation in every imaginable colour. And not just the trouser but the jacket too. No longer would it be a simple barrier against the dust of the desert and the unforgiving sun; now it would become a canvas on which the young and not so young could express their allegiance to various causes, combos, clubs and criminal gangs. Denim. God fabric. For the Demon God's people.

The Boozefighters MC never back down from a challenge. If you rev up your half-arsed machine in front of the pack, then you're asking for a winner-takes-fucking-all contest. So, when The Pissed Off Bastards let go the throttle and threw down the gauntlet, I happily picked it up. Mainstreet was mayhem, the squares were running for cover as we tore the tarmac up on our demobbed military Harleys. Screeching turns and wheelies drove regular drivers off the road. By nightfall the bars were nearly dry. Thirsty bikers scavenged for liquor, leading to stand-offs over scant resources. Some were in danger of sobering up and tensions were rising.

'Hey, pretty boy, what's that on your back?' I turned round to find the source of the taunting drawl. It was Stabby Keith of The Naughty Boys MC, a biker gang from Berdoo, California, comprised of ex-service personnel from the USAF field catering corp. Their sigil was crossed spoons under a demonic cake. I involuntarily turned round to check my back; I'd been time travelling a great deal that week and had momentarily forgotten what I was wearing. Ah, yes. Denim. I was paving the way for nascent biker chic. Having found the Californian sun a little too aggressive for my pallid Home Counties skin, I had customised my Wrangler 11MJ jacket by slicing of the sleeves and collar to make a makeshift vest. I had crudely etched the club's logo, a green bottle of booze, on to the back in fencing paint. I was decades ahead of the game, and I think I might have invented biker colours by mistake. It's often the way with us time travellers, stealing ideas from the future and passing them off as our own at an earlier date. It looked pretty cool, I thought – tough too. But I was still wearing a lurid floral shirt from 1969 and, of course, I had the rock and roll star's hair on under my Phrygian cap. This is what I presume had caused the pretty boy taunt, though simple inter-clan rivalry could not be completely ruled out.

'It's a sigil, dear boy, a bond, a mark of brotherhood and loyalty,' I replied to Stabby Keith with the air of an effete academic. Stabby Keith punched me full in the face with a leather-gloved fist. I rose from the Hollister dust and wiped the blood from my shattered nose. 'Don't fuck with the son of a Demon God,' I said, now more than a little inconvenienced. He spat on the floor and shuffled awkwardly from side to side like a drunken boxer. He came right up to my face, breathing acrid liquor fumes into my eyes.

'Want some more, pretty boy?' he growled.

I winced and wrinkled my nose. Stabby Keith was too tough to be dealt with by regular combat. This would require occult God power. Stepping one pace back and waving my hands like a children's party conjuror, I summoned the time vortex. It whirled into life on Hollister's main street, much to the surprise of the gathered motorcycle gangs. I nimbly directed the vortex with my magical fingers. It began to suck in Stabby Keith. He thrashed and lashed out at the invisible forces that were manipulating his body. He was lifted off the floor. With a swift click of my fingers the vortex reached its maximum velocity, drawing Stabby Keith into the time lanes. I had selected a suitable vehicle for my vengeance. Stabby Keith spun and buffeted by time found himself deposited into midst of the Battle of Kadesh in 1274 BC. He could take up his quarrel with the Hittites and Ramesses II. See where mocking this cat's garments gets you.

Back in Chaffinch-On-The-Hill I began to use denim as my signifier of non-conformity. Formally I had seen denims as merely a useful cloth to muck about in. It was flexible, hard-wearing and good for building camps in the woods. But as the counterculture began to inform my choices I took denim to be more of a holy raiment, like monks wearing habits or nun's wimples. Later I would wear it as a suit, waistcoat, pants and jacket. I had denim shoes, denim caps, denim bags, a denim wallet, denim handkerchiefs, denim shorts, denim underthings, denim pillowcases, denim duvets, books on denim, wall hangings depicting its history, framed photographs of the legs and asses of a thousand icons wearing God's fabric. I'd cover this book with denim if the publisher allowed me to. Washing denim is bad. It removes almost all of its sacred power. Detergent is the enemy of transcendence. This fitted nicely with my early heavy rock aesthetic. When my mother took me to Snazzy Chaps boutique I was horrified to find that new denim was, well, new. It had none of the grease and grime of the road that I was used to from my time in the Boozefighters MC. I kept the new generic brand denim jacket hidden deep within the Snazzy Chaps bag until I could get to work on it. I used my bicycle, the Red Baron. I ran over my new jacket repeatedly with its muddy tires. I rubbed it in the dirt and encouraged the family dog to make it into a temporary basket. I did everything in my power to uncork the magic I knew lay dormant in the threads that only dirt could summon. After patient hours of tactical tarnishing, the spell was finally successful. I added patches and badges, and in that moment when the last thread was sewn and the last pin clipped into place, a new gateway opened. I stepped back into the time vortex clad in robes of righteousness.

9

become a Machine

I spread a map out on my bedroom floor. It's a guide to hidden Home Counties portals. Places where I might be able access other dimensions. The bargain bins of NSS newsagents had been one such gateway, but there were others. I selected two likely spots that could be reached easily by public transport or by begging a lift from my mother. High Wycombe. Slough. Two urban locations with diverse populations with different tastes and desires, a break from the monocultural sterility of Chaffinch-On-The-Hill. Somewhere close to Eden before the fall, but with record shops. I made an altar from a pile of comics and a tea tray. I placed a saucer at its centre and lit the two tealights that I had placed on either side. I dug the Swiss army penknife my father had bought for me on his last business trip out of the pocket of my blue jeans. I opened the longest and sharpest blade. I passed the blade through the flame of the candles and held the glowing blade up to 'Hot From the Lock' by Flintlock in obeyance to the spirits of vinyl, whom I called upon to bless my quest. I sliced a gully into my thumb and let the blood drip into the saucer. I passed the flame over the pool of blood and watched it boil. The heat of the tealight fused the cut on my thumb and the wound vanished. I began to travel.

×

'You are, of course, aware that tinkering with time is the most heinous crime imaginable? A crime so foul that it remains one of the few felonies on the statute books that carries a sentence of immediate liquidation. There can be no allowance for nuance. No excuses. No pleas of ignorance. Because even the slightest alteration to the time continuum could result in unpredictable and disastrous outcomes. Intolerable tangents that could spell the end of all things. Even a single hair combed in the wrong direction may cause history to be rewritten in a most unfavourable manner. The unauthorised time traveller is an insufferable creator of paradox and contradiction and is a criminal by definition. The singular duty of humanity is to obey the laws of cause and effect. It is simple Newtonian physics. No quantum hocus-pocus is permitted here. You are not God, though you somehow fancifully claim to know the mind of God. Is it not the case that by simply making these statements in open court you are in fact admitting your guilt to the worst crime in history? Fomenting the end of history itself?'

The prosecutor is staring hard into the ceiling of the courtroom after delivering his furious rebuke. The jury members look at each other and shrug. He surely has his victory now. The room is quiet except for the occasional cough and the tap tap of journalists typing their reports into their tablets. The silence stretches. The judge looks at the young boy in the dock, expecting a reply. The response is not immediately forthcoming. The boy is smiling. He looks at the judge and gives him a cheeky wink.

×

Totality, infinity, rebirth. The sacred octagon. In AD 50 things are a little tricky. Caratacus, the leader of our people, has been defeated and taken back to Rome in chains. The legions of Emperor Claudius are building aqueducts and roads with impunity. Many of my fellow Catuvellauni have been crucified in the laybys of new Roman motorways. Everyone is feeling down. Not even the bard can revive our flagging spirits. I'm stood round a deep pit in what one day soon would be called High Wycombe with some of my fellow priests. We are weeping for our brother, the leader of our order, who was cruelly stabbed to death by a drunk centurion. An ironic end for Stabby Keith of the Naughty Boys MC, who had survived the Battle of Kadesh with most of his limbs intact but with a newfound sense of the futility of violence. He had taken holy orders, travelling back and forth through time, seemingly doing good and serving his community. At first I had been afraid that we might be doomed to repeat the punch-up we'd had in Hollister, but happily he greeted me with a cup of sweet mead and a warm embrace. We became firm friends, and I was soon initiated into his order: 'The Companions of the Sacred Blossom'. Petals rained down on the swaddled body of Stabby Keith as we sang sad incantations to our gods. Some half-cut Roman soldiers looked on, leaning on their spears, mocking our ceremony through the spring drizzle. I produced my Swiss army penknife from the folds of my robes and, after opening the scissors, trimmed some of my fingernails into the pit, thus guaranteeing the spirit of Stabby Keith would endure and blossom once again when the time came. And so it came to pass. The pit was filled, the grass grew, roots spread under the soil, a willow tree flourished on a small mound overlooking Stabby Keith's grave, its leaves fell, rotted and returned to the soil where the spirit of Stabby Keith rested, awaiting the summoning spell.

In October 1970 a vision of retail utopia sprung up in the sacred vale. High Wycombe. The Octagon Centre. At its heart was an octagonal glass-domed building two stories high, surrounded by pharmacies, card shops and bargain jewellery merchants. Under the paving stones at its very centre was the tomb of Stabby Keith. As the years rolled by and the portents multiplied, on the now-vanished mound where the willow tree once grew, a new temple was built. This new temple would house a new faith. The religion of the cyborg entity. The machine and the human. The temple's name was Percy Priors. Guitar shop. A purveyor of musical instruments that had risen from the amniotic sack of concrete and glass. The time was now. To that place at the appointed time, a conclave of adepts clad in denim robes bearing the insignia of their order made their solemn progress. The shop assistants bowed their heads and let out the holy sigh of resignation as the adepts entered and headed towards the electric guitars. I was amongst their number on that fateful day and was given the honour of selecting the instrument we would use in the summoning spell. I closed my eyes and let the spirit of the glade guide my hand. It came to rest on the neck of a Tokai Fender Stratocaster copy. I took it from its resting place and handed it to our master of the revels, a trainee troubadour by the name of Pete Bell Head, so named because of the Buddhist prayer bells he had tied in his hair that jingled and jangled as he walked. The shop staff now gathered around the altar/shop counter and uttered the opening prayer sacred to our order: 'Are you lot going to buy anything or what?'

'I would like a plectrum, my good man,' I offered in answer, as was our custom. The adepts laughed as Pete Bell

Head plugged in the Tokai. Suddenly there was silence. A hush like the sleep of the dead. Outside Boots the chemist the Skinheads bowed their heads. Cider was left undrunk. Punks sucked their gob back in and reflected on what the world might be like with more harmony and less conflict. Hell's Angels returned to hell to prepare for the rapture. Pete Bell Head struck the first chord. Dang! The waves of sound shook the panes of glass in the shop window, bending them like sails in a gale. Dang! A golden light spread throughout the shop. Dang!! Slightly atonal this time as Pete's fingers miss the appropriate frets. He looked up in panic. The ceremony must not be derailed now. I gave him a reassuring wink. He smiled back at me, his fingers now full of confidence. The chords began to flow. Dang! Dang! Dar! Dang, dang, dar dar! We began to pick up the words of the hymn, quietly at first, but then as Pete Bell Head's hands flap over the neck of the Tokai Fender Stratocaster copy like holy wings, we took off into the High Wycombe sky, our voices a broken chorus of teenage spirits: 'Smoke on the water, fire in the sky!'

And there is fire. Pete Bell Head is transformed into a hirsute Prometheus. Huge columns of flame that shoot out from the amplifier's speakers swirl around the shop and finally smash through the bowed windows of Percy Priors. Skinheads stare. Punks raise plastic bottles of snakebite. The fire forms into a great flaming arrow which plunges into the centre of the octagon: 'Smoke on the water, fire in the sky!'

Down through the soil of ages the fire cuts its relentless path. At last, its warmth passes through the mud and discarded crisp packets until it finds the body of Stabby Keith, still swaddled in his Catuvellauni robes. His dead eye sockets fill with light as the fire embraces him. The spirit of Stabby Keith is risen and suddenly there is music. Everywhere there is music! Punks kiss casuals, Teddy boys lie down with Skins, Mods make homes with Psychobillies, Oi Boys embrace Rastafari. Stabby Keith is risen, and the Octagon centre reveals its true purpose.

'Enough of that, you wankers, out, you're barred! You hear me? If you lot step in here again, I'll the call the police. Got it?' The shop assistants are reaching for the baseball bat they keep under the altar/counter. I call through the closing door, 'See you cats next week' and the ritual is complete.

A few months later and the promise of a bright future has receded, as all quixotic human projects tend to do. The ghost of Stabby Keith rides again, as the Naughty Boys MC opens a chapter in High Wycombe. His peaceful robes are thrown in a wheelie bin as he once again reverts to the roll of a nihilistic biker. The fucker let us all down. Its 1982 and I'm barefoot in the Octagon Centre. The revolution is in big trouble. 'The Land of Make Believe' by Bucks Fizz is straining out of a clothes shop's inefficient speakers. As a teenage representative of the counterculture, its saccharine lope is the crystallization of all I hate. I'm barefoot because I'm rejecting convention, man. I'm connecting with the vibrations of the planet, baby. I had given up my hand-stitched boots, the ones I had worn at the Mystic when Mason's grim fusillade came down, in the Wilderness, Manassas Gap, Chickasaw Bayou and Dove Creek. Kicking it with the Kickapoo. At Vimy Ridge, at Imjin River, at Culloden Field, at Dien Bien Phu, at Yalu River, at Carthage and the Milvian Bridge, in the neolithic caves, by the shores of Galilee. Now, my feet, bare as the day of my birth, would feel the cold concrete of municipal pavements and suck up the pools of spilt beer and vomit. My mother despaired, but I was doing it for all of us. Because if I failed to connect, then God would lay the whole damn thing to waste. Here, outside Boots the chemist. In metro land, in the desiccated remains of the United Kingdom. I'm out here looking for the source.

Bucks Fizz have won the culture war. They are playing on the tinny PA and their wild approximation of reggae is vexing me. The offbeat skank and wandering bass are present but incorrect. This is Thatcher's Britain, and the band are named after a yuppy cocktail. I couldn't hate it more. I'm barefoot because I reject the materialism of free market economics, man. Here on the plinth, a couple of yards down from Sainsburys. But I was wrong. One of the songwriters, Peter Sinfield, had already found its way into my home via the sprawling prog rock of King Crimson and, as it turns out, 'The Land of Make Believe' is a virulent attack on the policies of the Conservative administration. It's rebel music. It also contained a prophesy. *Time to change, Superman.*

The human spirit could be subverted and corrupted, but the music once created could not be destroyed. It was immortal and untameable. But where did music settle? Where could I gather it to me? Stabby Keith had opened doors that even his betrayal could not close again. One of these gateways lay at the source of the Oxford Road before the gates of West Wycombe and the Hellfire Caves. Scorpion records. Record shops. Temples. Church. Confessional. Laboratory. Record shops. The town became the incubator for a new kind of passion. A shameful love of the retail experience that somehow transcended the tawdry necessities of the supermarket, that was nothing like shopping for a new TV or picking out new school shoes. The newsagents of my home had been a pale imitation of these more profound structures. Where did the music settle? Record shops. Scorpion Records was a rudely furnished establishment run by two wizards. Jeff and Steg were in fact former members of 'The Companions of the Sacred Blossom'. After the fall of Caratacus they had left the tribe to travel the world in search of wisdom. They had gathered a treasure trove of second-hand vinyl from across the ages Stepping in, I was warmly greeted by my former brothers, and after engaging the secret handshake of our order, I was invited to browse the artefacts. My fingers began to flick restlessly through the stacks. To my untrained eye it was a confusing soup of words and images. This was where the music settled. The variety made my dizzy. I tried hard to remember the words on brother Jan's record sleeves. It was hard. They all had such lovely haircuts and the artwork on the sleeves was a pure kaleidoscope of human imagination. I had to step back for a moment, take a breath, focus the vibration. Record shops. Where machines sing.

My inexpert hands fumbled over sleeves. Dragging titles out. Trying to analyse with no frame of reference. I trusted in chaos and God's guidance. Echoes of words from Jan's enthusiastic phone conversations began to combine with the record sleeves. *Five Man Army* by Dillinger, Trinity, Wayne Wade, Al Campbell, and Junior Tamlin, *Shut me Mouth* by Ranking Dread, *Soon Forward* by Gregory Isaacs, *One Common Need* by Lincoln Thompson & The Rasses. A/B, B/C condition, all for less than £10. Brother Jan had uttered the first lines of spell a few weeks ago on a crackly phone line from Uppsala polytechnic. Jah Stitch. Prince Jazzbo. King Tubby. Lee. Scratch. Perry. Now the ritual was unfolding, just as he said it would. I found myself in a cloudy studio. It was filled with smoke, decorated with symbols and icons, and it was shaking to the sound of the future.

Then it began. Evolution. The voice of mutation revealing itself. Creation is the birth of something new from something familiar. Drums. Bass. Horns. Guitar. The human voice. Rearranged into fantastic new patterns. It's 1973. In Europe and the USA millionaire rockers are trying to rinse the last drop of originality out of the delta blues that they casually stole more than a decade ago. Expensive studios.

State of the art. But here, in this place, wizards are making machines speak. Instantly, everything else now sounds ridiculously trite. Invention flourishes when resources are scarce. The line between Scientist, King Tubby, Keith Hudson, the Great Upsetter and hazy mornings lying under friends' tables in the aftermath of an acid house happening is drawn. I can hear it in the acid tracks, in the garage dubs, in Bobby Konders, The Moody Boys, The Orb, Renegade Soundwave, Greater Than One, Guerrilla records, Bristolian beats, The Original Rockers, The Idjut Boys, Faze Action, Andrew Weatherall. I can sense its presence in Bauhaus, PIL, The Members, Ruts DC, The Flying Lizards, Sula Bassana, Talking Drums, ESG, Liquid Liquid, Saada Bonaire. In the Lijadu Sisters, Chouk Bwa & The Angstromers, Bro Valentino, Brother Resistance, Desmond Chambers, The Mebusas. In Codek, X- Certs, Ponty Mython, Kasai Allstars, Persian, Ty Lumnus. In every record where wide-open space is allowed and where the machine helps the music expand into the gaps. All this sound is mind mediated through mechanism.

Humans are toolmakers. Stone axes, sling shots, shotguns, stylus and turntable, synthesiser. But once created, these tools will take on lives of their own beyond all attempts to control or guide them. All purpose is lost, all intention forgotten. Sometimes you can clearly see the machine controlling the human. At other times it's more like the creation of a man-machine hybrid, where wits and wires are locked in a kind of perpetual stand-off with neither side able to claim dominance. This was acid house. The fusion of tool and operator, where the roles were interchangeable. Cheap bits of kit make history; they connect the frailty of flesh to the atomic flow. Punk rock technology. The four-track tape, the Grampian reverb and the Echoplex tape delay. The Roland 303. The 303, a cheap shit bassline machine. But in its plastic shell it held potent magic. It took a fallible, hungry human mind to unlock that magic. Driven by economic necessity, the 303 had made its way to the bargain basement. Out of production. Unloved. Useless. In 1980s Chicago DJ Pierre heard Jasper play a bassline on this little unloved module. Spanky picked one up for pence. The machine was so happy to be off the shelf and out of its box again it went wild. It was like a bucking stallion, or a penned-up cow released on to the spring lawn. No one could control it; all they could do was record its new song and let the revolution unfold. But I'm getting ahead of myself here. I forget you are not all time travellers. Apologies.

In 1982, in Scorpion Records, I picked up a record that captured this struggle between machine and man. A record selected via some distantly recalled conversation with an older boy with an attractive tour patch bearing the legend Tangerine Dream. This was my initiation into the birth of tragedy, the juxtaposition of order and chaos, Apollo and Dionysus, Edgar Froese, Peter Bauman and Christopher Franke engaged in cyborg relations. A sequencer, seeking the balance between the regularity of formalised notation and the irrational passion of circuits. The glow of the Tangerine Dream. Barely contained fountains of notes pitter-pattered on a bed of eerily extended ethereal drones. I was thrown into the depths of space, the bottom of the ocean, the heart of the sun. I was elsewhere but ever-present. Throughout time, as I travelled on my quest, the sound of the sequencer would weave its way around my cortex, pulsing out its reassuring signal. From that moment on, machines would be my unpredictable companions.

On my way back to the Octagon I bumped into God, who was picking out a birthday card for Asmodeus, one of the kings of hell. They hadn't spoken for a while and God wanted to get him something nice this year by way of a peace offering. They were going to Santo's place later for a barbeque. God had made a mixtape with some of the numbers I'd picked out for her, which she hoped would help break the ice.

God's Mixtape for Asmodeus's Birthday Party

Side One

1. Fiery Jack – The Fall
2. Spooky Nuisance – Satan's Satyrs
3. USA/USB – Ultra Satan
4. Devil Gate Drive— Suzi Quatro
5. Devil Devil – Tonetta

6. Devil Got My Woman – Skip James

7. Devil's Pickney – Sugar Minott

8. Friend of the Devil – Grateful Dead

9. That Ole Devil Called Love – Billie Holiday

10. Race With The Devil – Gene Vincent

11. Will of the Devil – Moon Duo

12. Synth is Not Love (Benge Dub) – Black Devil Disco Club

13. Angels and Demons at Play – Sun Ra

Side Two

1. Devil's Anvil – Eddie Warner

2. Carnival of Souls – The Verbtones

3. Demon Hit – Extra Classic

4. Some Kind of Demon – Gong, Gong, Gong

5. Shake Off the Demon – Brewer & Shipley

6. Little Demon – Screamin' Jay Hawkins

7. It's Alright Ma, It's Only Witchcraft – Fairport Convention

8. The Witch – Large Plants

9. Thou Shalt Not Cry – Witch

10. She's My Witch – Kip Tyler

11. Lucifer – The Salt

12. Hell or Heaven – L.U.P.O

13. The Devil's Own – David Sylvian

'Great tape, God, some nice sounds on there – glad you dug those tunes I sent you. I'm not sure I've heard that Large Plants one before.'

'Thanks, Jonah, and thanks for the tunes, man. Yeah, Large Plants are new, man, a beat combo out of Bedford, fuzz pedal necromancers with a cool twin guitar attack channelling a bit of early Deep Purple, Zeppelin and a hint of Bert Jansch on the vocals. Least that's what I got out of it.' God looked wistful; even supreme beings could be transported by a good tune.

'Yes, yes, I'm feeling it. Hey, I've just been browsing in Scorpion Records, and I think I've found my calling.' I was feeling evangelical about the bag of records I'd scored.

'Oh, really?' God says. 'Sounds good, man, let's have a look.'

There was *Phaedra* by Tangerine Dream, *Rainbow Dome Musick* by Steve Hillage, a 12-inch by an unknown techno artist using numbers where words normally stood, The Tom Tom Club, disco records that blended the sound of outer space with the sweat of freedom's basement. There was Kraftwerk and Boogie Down Productions, there was a mind-meld from Johnny Spaceship, a self-conscious AI programme from the twenty-second century. There was the output of a thousand bedroom studios and a thousand future dance floors. There was the humble pile of the King's music. Dubwise.

God checks the titles and nods approvingly at the selection.

'God,' I say, hands on hips and with my face pointing to the future, 'when I grow up, I want to become a machine.'

10

Slough and the serpent Messenger

There's a generosity to the universe. It's always creating new ways of being, new configurations that fuse to create fresh unexpected objects. It's a constant becoming. To nowhere. To no-thing. There's a generosity amongst the gods that often goes unremarked amidst all the smiting and laying waste to sinners. Bestowing unto so-and-so this and that special power. Great beauty. Great strength. Great fucking riffs. My favourite God-given capacity was the power of trans-dimensional space travel. By the simple application of my imagination and the blood of my flesh, I was able to cross vast distances and disparate time zones almost instantaneously. Nothing gives one a better perspective on the fragility of mankind than a trip around the vast emptiness of space. To witness a galaxy explode into being. To watch a star implode with quiet dignity. These events are of such magnitude that they crush any pretentions of human significance as surely as the dark heart of a black hole annihilates all the follies that cross its path. Meanwhile, back on Earth, we grope about in our own limited way, creating stories to try and account for our disconnection. That was the cruellest gift of all. Impatient, faulty consciousness. Human consciousness. Pitifully ill-formed and directionless, like an infant seeing all things through its own inadequate eyes. With mankind at the centre, a full fifty percent of all that exists. Us, and everything else. What a withered ontology that is. But there exist a few enlightened pioneers who, through will and mind-expanding substances alone, attempt to bend the bars of the cage. Such a group of radical free-thinkers operate from inside the spaceship Hawkwind. A living biological vessel crewed by cyborg hybrids masquerading as a space-rock pop combo. The sound of Hawkwind is a post-apocalyptic sonic terror device combined with a prophetic early warning system. Their music is the noise of civilisation unravelling. The soundtrack to a burning barricade. A beautiful nightmare trance.

In the early years of the 1980s I was living in the early 1970s. That's to say, while my body was being pulled apart by the raging hormones of my teenage years, my mind and dress sense had been transported to a squat in Ladbroke Grove in 1972 where they were happily living an approximation of the counterculture, but with microwave ovens. While my schoolfriends perfected wedges and channelled the thrill of 'Thriller' or the early stirrings of hip-hop, I was listening to space madrigals and wore anachronistic clothes excessively laden with patchouli oil. The horror on the face of the young assistant at Snazzy Chaps of Chaffinch-On-The-Hill when I asked if they stocked flares is an image I shall never erase. But like all good time travellers, I was never anchored in one place or time zone for long. I was simultaneously hanging out in the Black Ark with Lee Perry and the Revolutionaries, on my way to Prestwich with Mark E. Smith and The Fall, whilst still finding time to visit the Zodiak Free Arts Lab in West Berlin where my lifelong friend Edgar Froese and I tried to fracture the Berlin Wall with a bank of sequencers.

Back in 1982, I began to receive signals. Like morse code, but with strangely elongated tones that seemed to last a lifetime. Bleep, bip, dah, dang. Under the code was a relentless changing chug. Drums chattering. A single note played over and over again. Ritual music. The Hawklords and their space pirate horde. The notes contained a map, a star chart guiding my lost parts back to the source. A nihilistic sentinel. I packed up my Adidas school bag with all the necessary equipment, barre chords, heavy plectrums, Barney Bubbles graphics and Moorcock anthologies. I followed the drang and clang, down Damnation Alley, onto the edge: the edge of time. The signals led me back to Earth. Having expected to be transported to the outer reaches of Andromeda, I was slightly disappointed when my star charts revealed the rendezvous point to be the Slough Fulcrum Centre on the spiral arm of the B416.

Slough does not have a reputation as a wellspring of occult knowledge, but then, like all good psychic nodes, it hides its secret well. It is in fact home to several portals into other dimensions. My mother worked as a chef at one such gateway. Those familiar with the comedy show *The Office* may well recall the opening credits where a panning shot takes in the horizons of Slough roundabout, the bus station and the putative headquarters of the office. A modest dull grey tower block constructed in the careless brutalist style of a bygone age. What many viewers did not realise is that this was a transmitter for talking to God. Divine transmitters are almost always disguised as everyday objects. This dissuades amateurs from bothering the gods with their inane requests. In this particular dimension the transmitter was manifested as the head office of a compressed air company. 'Nothing compares to COMPAIR' was their catchy slogan. I had become keenly attuned to the hidden world and so, of course, realised its true function.

COMPAIR tower had great views. From its executive dining room, you could see way past the bus station and roundabout, out over the dual carriageway, almost to the outskirts of Eton. Before the management team sat down to enjoy the lunch my mother had prepared, I was allowed access to this exclusive observation post. I used the time wisely, setting up small altars using moss and gunk from the gutters. I carved runes in the dust with a knife I had stolen from the COMPAIR executive cutlery set. I looked out over the rooftops of the bus station and waited for a sign. For weeks I repeated my ritual, gradually adding complexity to the rites. I cut myself with my father's Swiss army penknife, the one he had given me in the hope of stirring some affinity with woodcraft from my stubbornly unpractical hands. This was by now a familiar ritual act for me, my fingers crisscrossed with scars from various summonings and time travel expeditions. I let the blood drip from the latest cut onto the makeshift moss altar and waited, but still no signal. Perhaps my instincts about the relative psychic conductivity of this grey office block were wrong. Suddenly I felt a sensation in my pocket. Not an unusual occurrence for a boy of my age. But this stirring had a different quality to it. It was if something were trying to escape. Something alive, wild and writhing. Sharp pricks like viper bites punctured my skin; the sensation was excruciating. In the kitchen my mother chopped carrots. On the balcony of COMPAIR, Nirah the messenger, serpent god of Mesopotamia, like the head piece of Crowley's Thelemic headpiece come to life, had dematerialised in the pocket of my Wrangler cords.

As I held the writhing snake in my teenage hands, the landscape of Slough was transformed into a great trans-dimensional blueprint, revealing gateways, portals and nodes of power. Nirah the serpent hissed and pointed with its forked tongue, flicking it towards points of interest. I hurriedly made a mental note of all the sites of maximum cosmic connectivity before the executives arrived for their lunch.

Site 1: Slough Indoor market badge and patch shop

Between the fruit and veg stalls, round the corner from a fishmonger and the town's sole *Defender* machine, lay a gateway to a variety of times and places run by a man made almost entirely of nicotine and disrepute. He was more than likely on any number of police watch lists judging by his choice of magazine stock. But he cared little for the law. He was a dark wizard from a long line of guardians whose duty it was to distribute fetishes to the young and adventurous. He said little, and those words he did offer were chosen for their expletive punch rather than their elucidatory power. But such is the way with gurus. Misunderstood and misinterpreted. His stall was ostensibly a newsstand. He did indeed stock papers. Books also. Special books. Special magazines. Hidden behind plastic from the prying eyes of curious children. But I was not called there by Nirah the messenger for smut. I came for patches and badges. Whenever funds were sufficient, I would head to the market and study the boards where the badges hung like martyrs on gibbets. Such an array of artists. Some with familiar names, others a total mystery. This is where art, capitalism, music and magic collided. Badges and patches, part advertising hoarding, part sigil. I would let aesthetics guide me; pleasing or challenging images that would excite a reaction in my school friends were my first purchases. Instant cool rendered in tin. Badges came first, then hastily made cassettes of their work borrowed from brother Jan or taped off the radio. These were risky times. School friends might call your bluff. Name your favourite five songs by Krokus then. Metal Rendezvous, it was cheap. But risks taken often yield lifelong bonds or salient warnings. The new wave of British heavy metal was not for me, despite its attractive iconography. So, the spectrum narrowed and the focus sharpened. It was flower power space rock, barefoot and beautiful. One by one I added the shiny talismans to my jacket like a voodoo priest pricking a poppet. Sabbath, Zeppelin's runic symbols, the Dead, the Planet Gong, Tangerine Dream, Here & Now, Hawkwind, but also Misty in Roots and Gregory Isaacs, alongside a sprinkling of groups with logos that far outshone their musical output. These symbols transported me to new dimensions. They were markers on a path that led to music.

Site 2: Our Price

The badges held power. They directed me in strange, unexpected ways. In search of space. But finding instead *Linton Kwesi Johnson in Dub*. On sale, in my bag, and soon shaking the foundations of Rouge Mount Road as my neighbours trimmed the lawn. Nirah the messenger writhed and wriggled. The letter R. The Canadian prog power trio Rush, but behind *A Farewell to Kings*, where the badge had initially directed me, was Roxy Music. Risqué covers. Risky music. Check the credits. Vibe off Eno and Ferry. Find the Warm Jets. The bargain bins hold gold. Sports hall-filling rock gods fallen on hard times release disappointing fifth album. 99p. But that's where the treasure is buried. From pre-denim Quo to Dillinger does disco. We make beauty from the waste. Repurpose the landscape, like Lance Mountain riding a storm drain. Beyond the Top 40. Beyond taste and best-of lists, where the limits of cash-strapped youth force the gems from hiding. Years later we call it Balearic.

Site 3: Tubs Marin's Fingers

Odysseus returning home from the liquidation of Troy took something of a circuitous route. Seduction, cyclops and sirens. The lethargy of the Lotus Eaters. But his greatest challenge came not from mythical beasts cursed by the gods, or from soporific songs and sorcery, but from the *Defender* console in Slough market. There are many heroes of antiquity; some I have had the pleasure to know, others were friends of friends or passing acquaintances on nodding terms at social functions. But few remained as mysterious to me as Odysseus, or as he was known in 1982 ... Tubs Marin. I was not a skilled fighter, having decided on pacifism instead of active conflict. I was particularly inept in the field of digital combat. In the days before home computers and games consoles, the only place one could become a gladiator was in the foyers of cinemas, pubs and randomly situated modules like the *Defender* machine in Slough market. But like the carcass of an antelope freshly slain, it was the biggest and strongest who got the first pickings. Tough lads. Blokes with motorbike helmets. Cigs dangling from frowning gobs. I would watch over their shoulders and dream of being a gunnery operative. Slough market daytime weekdays was not a time for tough lads – they had part-time jobs – but for us young ones it was the one time we might make it on to the scoreboard. Dizzi had skills with his wrists; he could flick and tickle the joystick, his trigger finger pumping the button as he cleared the skies of alien invaders. Dizzi was the Chaffinch-On-The-hill *Defender* champion, and I was his aide-de-camp. We made our way to the market. Scored a few badges and counted out our change. The stench of dead fish on ice signalled our arrival at the arena. The *Defender* machine lay opposite the fishmonger, next to a stall selling cheap radios. It was unattended. Dizzi flipped the coins into the slot and the display lit up. The fighting was hard. Many good pilots perished. But the battle was finally won, and with a handsome tally too. The leader board scrolled up. Dizzi and I were confident of a high ranking; it was one of his best scores.

1. Tubs Marin
2.Tubs Marin
3.Tubs Marin
4.Tubs Marin
5. Dizzi

This was our first encounter with the champion. The summer holidays were long and our visits frequent. Once, Dizzi penetrated the Top Three only to find himself relegated to Ten by the relentless power of Tubs Marin's fingers. Franky Fucks entered and was dispatched. Jen, super slink, Fozzy bear, Carol with a K, Giant, Noddy, Wingnut. Never more than bit part players, whose brief appearance on the scoreboard was nothing more than a temporary inconvenience. There were no serious challengers to Tubs Marin's supremacy. Some of the high scores were scarcely believable. Like *The Iliad*, their fame was recounted orally in the bus shelters of the county. Wherever teenager, cigarette and cheap lager were joined, so the tale of Tubs Marin's high scores would be told. Dizzi and I took to long hours of patient surveillance, lurking in the fruit and veg, hoping to catch a glimpse of the fabled warrior. But they were never seen. Not even a hint of their passing. Some of the older stall holders claimed to have seen him. She was an air force fighter pilot home on leave. He was seven feet tall with muscles like a weightlifter. She was short and unremarkable dressed in a snorkel parka. He was an ace-face like Sting in *Quadrophenia*. She was a woman for all seasons, an 'every' person, a universal being, a monad of all that ever was or shall ever be. Only their name etched in pixelated characters on a screen provided any clue to their existence. Humanity needs stories to live, things to aspire to that make the longing tangible. Tubs Marin was a magical being no less than the Minotaur or the Phoenix. He or she or they. Tubs was all of them, a sexless champion. Unbeatable, unattainable perfection.

Site 4: Slough Fulcrum Centre

Nirah's forked tongue settled on the canopy of the Queensmere Shopping Centre. It's obsidian eyes like dark jewels glinted in the Berkshire sunlight. 'It is time,' it hissed. As black as space and as deranged as an astronaut lost in its vast emptiness. The Valium drone of society collapsing. De-evolution. Revolution. Nothing. No-when. Hawkwind. The tribe was gathered, the robes were selected. I chose a lab coat. Dave Brock, the taciturn but steady captain of spaceship Hawkwind favoured them as stage attire, and who was I to argue with Dr Technical. I had crudely stencilled the cover of *Choose Your Masques*, the long player to which this tour was dedicated, on the back of the lab coat in suitably cosmic silver pen. I looked fucking ridiculous. But then they say that about all visionaries.

Pints in plastic cups that bend in the middle like unformed clay on a potter's wheel: I'm holding for the tribe. The crew is tight, dedicated to the cause. Dizzi. Me. The Wisdom, a hip cat from the southlands with a buckskin fringed jacket, a Byrds haircut, beanpole legs, and a love of the esoteric arts. Pat Gloom, a substantially proportioned dude and lead lute player in a quasi-mediaeval beat combo called The Pageants, he's a bit older than us and usually scores the cigs. You can smoke in this dimension. We are young, so we go at it. I'd tried to smoke hops on the bus over, but it just made me sick. The driver tried to throw us off, said that we'd been burning compost. Dizzi has a bit of red Leb, which goes great with cheap lager. We are giggling. There are older cats here, peace convoy types, Hell's Angels, some anarcho-punks with Crass stencils and even a handful of new wave kids, hip to the motoric sound. We are in the bar of the Slough Fulcrum Centre and Brian Tawn is selling *Hawkfan* fanzines. We buy merch. Proper screen-printed numbers with tour dates on the back. Dizzi points out the date on the back.

'See this, this is history right here,' he says.

'Yeah, Dizzi, it is. Here and now. Between Chippenham Golddiggers and Nottingham Rock City.'

I add the exact time and space coordinates. We can hear the support band striking up. Let's get to the front. No one likes support bands for some reason. But tonight, it's something special, a super group consisting of members of Can, Amon Düül, Cluster, Kraftwerk, Phuture, Stereolab, Sula Bassana, Black Mountain, Paternoster, Al Lover, Cybotron, Kuunatic and 808 State. We are right down the front as the Slough Fulcrum dissolves and becomes the Thunderdome, *Frenzy* in Blackpool, the back of a truck in a field, a beach as dawn breaks with Choci and Harvey working the mixer, my living room two days in, the cellar of an unremarkable Mancunian terrace with sedated ravers attached to monitors. The motor trance of ages. We all get down, passing the red Leb and sipping our lager from flexible cups. The support band play for maybe two weeks, hard to say, but they cover a lot of ground musically.

'They were pretty good, I thought. Something like the future,' I opined, passing the hot embers of the spliff to one of my comrades.

'Let's score some speed from those bikers,' suggests The Wisdom.

Speed helps you focus. The Wisdom tries to buy it off a guy he knows from High Wycombe. He's Windsor Hell's Angel adjacent, terrifying, with a shaved head and a woven plat at the back like a fucking Viking warrior. Goes by the name of 'Seedy Sid'. But Seedy Sid's prices are excessive, so The Wisdom returns empty handed. The collective looks unhappy. I eye Seedy Sid from across the bar. Ripped jeans over leathers all covered in oil. He's drinking snakebite in prodigious quantities. He'll need a piss soon, and with all those layers on he'll definitely use a cubicle to disrobe, plus it's a good opportunity for a sniff in peace. As suspected, Seedy Sid makes for the toilets. I jump up and head there too. The crew watch me with some apprehension. I smile back weakly and signal 'no sweat'. In the toilet the stench is primal, like the latrine of hell. 'After you mate, I'm waiting.' I usher pissers forward. Seedy Sid is just in front of me. Waiting. A spiky haired youth in a Conflict T-shirt spills out of a cubicle and gives Seedy Sid a curled punk rock snarl. Seedy Sid would have punched him out or worse but he's on probation. In he goes. I follow behind.

'What you doing, cunt? Fuck off or I'll knock you out.' His eyes are bulging from his rat-like face, which is criss-crossed with knicks and scars. Seedy Sid has surprisingly minty breath as he shouts in my pimply face. His face is a jumble of anger and confusion. My purpose is obscure to him; is it lust or larceny that has driven me to invade the cubicle? He reaches for the knife he has hidden under his cut-off. My hand shoots out and grips his arm. I hold him tight. I smile at him and shrug my shoulders. 'Sorry about this.' I look him in the eye as my suckers unfurl from my body. Seedy Sid looks like a confused child. For a second I feel something like regret. But it passes. I feel no shame as I liquidate him with my vampire suckers. He begins to shrivel like a deflating balloon. As he shrinks I help myself to the contents of his pockets. He has an exciting variety of pills and powders. Some I recognise. Some are of a more esoteric nature. There is one bag different from the others. It's not the usual polythene baggy but looks more like it's made from flexible frosted glass. Inside the bag, a blood red powder catches my eye. It has the air of a forbidden sacrament. I shudder slightly and have a vague premonition of a mass poisoning. This is not something one should take lightly. Certainly not at a Hawkwind concert. I carefully separate the red powder bag from the others and stash it safely in my lab coat. Seedy Sid is shrinking fast. Soon he is no more than a fleshy flap. I flush him down the toilet and leave the cubicle. Now wash your hands.

We become one singled-minded entity. We must fuse the open-ended structure of space rock with the militant energy of dance. Seedy Sid's amphetamine cocktail is taking effect. We are back in the auditorium gyrating to the hum of the PA. The lights go down. My skull throbs. The now-dark interior of the Fulcrum Centre is outer space. A strange siren sound emanates from the dark. Bleep, blip, swoosh. Modulated tones snake around the speakers. Nirah's tongue flickers and hisses. There is a drone building under the skittering beeps. My brain starts to pick up signals. The drone is reaching a bone-crushing intensity. Suddenly a massive spaceship swoops in through the skylight. The spaceship Hawkwind. The stage lights up like the deck of an interstellar craft. The crew shuffle onto the flight deck. Lank-haired operatives, silent and purposeful. From out of the immense drone the chug-chug-chug of a riff begins to tear the fabric. It's mesmerising. We are floating in space, awaiting the end of all things, when a maniac with a shaved head painted white, a foot-long bright green hair spike jutting from the front, dressed in a harlequin patterned bodysuit, roller-skates onto the stage blowing atonal blasts from a saxophone. This is Nik Turner. The spirit of Hawkwind and all revolutionary acts. Time has no meaning anymore: this is speed-charged hyper time. The set is a blur of notes, maybe just one note, stretched over days. They play 'Ejection' and 'The Right Stuff', two Calvert numbers that sound like the Cold War condensed into an overheated valve. 'Spirit of the Age'. 'Shot Down in the Night'. 'Brainstorm'. 'Master of the Universe'. When that final riff starts up, I catch sight of God basking in the strobe light's pulse. She grins at me and spins around like a whirlwind in the desert. The Master of the fucking Universe.

Mixtape for Seedy Sid's Deflated Corpse

Side One

1. Damnation Alley – Hawkwind
2. Master Builder – Gong
3. Old Danube – Paternoster

4. *Dead Mantra – Dead Skeletons*

5. *Garbage – The Deviants*

6. *Fresh Garbage – Spirit*

7. *Making Time – The Creation*

8. *Paradox – Lacewing*

9. *Supernaut – Black Sabbath*

10. *9 – Föllakzoid*

11. *Gulf of Lost Souls – Hedersleben*

12. *Time Centre – Michael Moorcock & The Deep Fix*

13. *Roundabout – Yes*

Side Two

1. *Lucifer Sam – Pink Floyd*

2. *It Just Won't Be That Way – The Gurus*

3. *What You See Is What You Get – Here & Now*

4. *Sploosh! – Ozric Tentacles*

5. *Objectoism, Objectonao – Gal Costa*

6. *Raj Neesh – Inner City Unit*

7. *Cycle-Delic – Davie Allan & The Arrows*

8. *Bat Macumba – Os Mutantes*

9. *Cardboard Pile – Kikagaku Moyo*

10. *Phom Rak Mueang Thai – Khun Narin*

11. *Ejection – Robert Calvert*

12. *Inward Turning Suns – The Holy Family*

13. *It's All Too Much – Steve Hillage*

11

Northolt hold-up

The ambulance siren whines in the distance as other concerned colleagues and members of the court crowd around a fallen juror. This is not the first time testimony in this case has caused one of the jury members to suffer a seizure. The judge's arthritic hand is aching from his constant hammering of the gavel on the bench. The defence team is flicking through a brochure for canal breaks on the Norfolk Broads. The young defendant waves and smiles to his supporters in the gallery. There is a festive spirit in the courtroom. The chief prosecutor is pacing up and down as he tries to maintain the momentum of a case which is being constantly interrupted by vomiting and collapse. He pauses to rest his hand on the teetering pile of books on the table. A tower of titles that make up Jonah Plantagenet's literary career. This is prosecution exhibit 2001.

×

I'm incapable of original thought. Every word I write, every word you read, is stolen from the aeons-old lexicon of human signs and signifiers. I am a thief, a highway robber of sentences and snappy phrases. Everyone is. We are all notorious felons. Send us down, dear judge, for we are all guilty as charged. Every term, every idiom, every idea, relies on a chaotic web of previous ideas. Every thought committed to speech or paper is connected to a network of actors both flesh and stone that stretches back to the first moment. God had the primary, and only, original thought; and that was nothing. We, however, cannot think of a single thing without the thing itself. Nothing is separate or alone. Nothing is true because we say it is. Truth is decided in the parliament of all things. We are merely intermediaries for the ever withdrawn and hidden universe. All of humanity's claims of original thought are spurious. There is no such thing as genius. All human thought is parasitic. The true hero in the story of Archimedes' eureka moment was the bath.

There is a Christian bookshop about halfway down the Silver Mound in Chaffinch-On-The-Hill. Its name is Herod's Seed Cafe. It's a modest two-tiered establishment with a tea room up top and a gift shop selling holy bric-a-brac at street level. No one has ever shoplifted from this store because no one would want anything in it. It does well because it is the only cafe in the village. The staff are faultlessly polite, and their cakes are of a consistently high standard. This is where the future of radical postmodern literature will be stolen and sold on. Not the Left Bank, the Sorbonne, Joyce's Dublin, the East Village, the West Village, the British Library, Tokyo, Delhi, or Northolt's Western Avenue, but here, in Herod's Seed Cafe. This is where I began to turn pretension into prose, with the help of blood and chicanery. Alongside the transcendent capacity of sound, I had a growing awareness of the power of words. They existed, not only as commands uttered by teaching staff or angry parents, but they also had a more benevolent occult function. They were not simply things to be copied down and memorised by rote. Arranged in a certain order, words had the power to transform reality itself. To bend time, to create new entities that, once born, went on to change other things in their turn. Words were the conjuring spell. The magic that made the confusion of living bearable. Vehicles for travel more efficient than any car or aeroplane. I could be in the islands of Japan coming of age in a remote fishing village in the morning and the halls of an alien monarch's throne room in the afternoon. Words. Fucking words, man. There was violence, redemption, horrible prejudice, empathy, sexual energy, religious fervour, the deepest contemplation and the most harrowing betrayal in words. All life was here. All life and new life, unimagined life, death and beyond death. These were the signs of humanity's desperate clawing, like the scratches on the inside of a coffin. The Demon God's demented gift to the universe. Stories.

My literary growth moved in lockstep with my developing musical tastes, and those first steps were purely escapist. The radical tedium of life on Rouge Mount Road drove my games to wild extremes of fantasy. The house porch was a castle besieged by revolutionary forces intent on overthrowing the corrupt regime. I would play either faction of the conflict depending on what side of the imperialist fence I landed on. Sometimes brave defender of tradition and order, other times insurgent guerrilla fighting to liberate the people. Either way, like all good soldiers, I would end up lying on the front lawn, dead with my tongue hanging out and a stick held to my chest to signify a bayonet, spear, or arrow, until it was time for dinner. The woods were the home of ghosts, zombies, or the lungs of a monster. Trees were knights in armour or leaders of an inscrutable alien race. Rouge Mount Road itself, its very tarmac, was a river to be forded or an invisible barrier between worlds. The first books I got into were extensions of this fantasy world. Elric or Dorian Hawkmoon and all the fantastic worlds of Michael Moorcock. Hawkwind were wanderers in this new province; the further I travelled with them through the cold wastes, the more of their reading habits I picked up. Moorcock was their literary muse, his words scattered across their music on *Warrior on the Edge of Time, Space Ritual, Sonic Attack*, and the Hawkwind-adjacent Deep Fix. I dug out the references and sought out the books. But all this sword and sorcery led me to deeper dimensions too. Moorcock's amoral adventurer Jerry Cornelius became a role model. A shapeshifting time traveller with scant regard for convention was something to aspire to. Moorcock's universe provided the psychic scenery for my teen fever dreams. I tripped through the never-ending party scene in the Final Programme, felt the claustrophobic madness of the Black Corridor, walked the streets of Mother London, and heard the voice of the Whispering Swarm. Hawkwind's most intriguing occasional member was a South African-born, Kent-dwelling fellow time traveller called Robert Calvert. He too was on a mission from God. He had long forgiven me for my earlier assault on his person in Meanwhile Gardens and we had become firm friends. We would often meet in strange, unexpected places: a cafe under the Great Pyramid, a dive bar on Venus where Herr Stuber was DJing, or the cockpit of a Sopwith Strutter over Ypres. He would talk incessantly, expounding his wild theories on everything from the rules of robotics, the nature of lycanthropy, or the contents of an Australian doctor's medicine cabinet. He was a new wave auteur, a proto-punk rock hero and a sharp social observer who could peel back the layers of nonsense and drown the world in his absurdist poetry. His words led to a great expansion of my bookshelves, from song titles and the hidden codes of his lyrics

I found Herman Hesse, James Blish, Roger Zelazny, Robert Heinlein, Alfred Jarry, Asimov, J.G. Ballard.

J.G Ballard was pulling out of a layby just past the RAF Northolt aerodrome where the royal family liked to touchdown incognito. He was heading west towards the A40 and the Hillingdon dry ski slope. I'm riding parallel to his Jaguar coupe on a souped-up Honda motorbike. I look in through the passenger window through the rain-spattered lenses of my motorcycle goggles. There he is, concentrating on the road, thinking up plots for new motor age stories. Where concrete, steel and wheel merge into one grotesque cybernetic organism. He looks like a suave barrister, hair swept back vampire-like, denying his encroaching baldness as a warlock denies the devil on the rack. He is unaware of my presence, as I'm not, strictly speaking, there. It's 1971. *Hunky Dory* has been released and Chris Squire has just funked up 'Roundabout' by Yes. There's beauty trying to assert itself against the backdrop of 1970s decline. Ballard is dreaming erotic dreams of motor cars and surgery. I want it. I want to be him. I must be him. I must be the most celebrated author of my generation. Challenging but entertaining. Absurd but plausible. Satirical. Horrifying. Hideous. Sensual. I must be him *now*. I turn the Honda directly into the path of his custard yellow Jag. Ballard is safety conscious. Despite the images of twisted metal running through his brain, he has no wish to mutilate me or himself, so he swerves. But he's going too fast, and my incursion into his path is too insistent, so, just shy of the roundabout, he collides with a lamppost. There are no witnesses; I made sure of that by subtly shifting the road on to a plane where road transport has been abolished. I slow the Honda and pull in just in front of the wreckage. I walk towards the smouldering pile, removing my motorbike helmet as I go. The car is fucked; the bonnet is crumpled and bent, with steam escaping from the interior like an angry dragon. The windscreen is shattered where J.G. Ballard's head has impacted the glass. Inside, the celebrated author is in bad shape, blood pouring from his pulverised features, nose on the wrong part of his face. His teeth look shattered. I reach in through the broken driver-side window and feel for a pulse. It's weak but present. He'll live, but he'll require major reconstruction. I deploy my vampire suckers and steal the plots for *Crash*, *High Rise*, *Running Wild*, *Cocaine Nights*, *Kingdom Come* and *Super Cannes*. I leave him some short stories and *Empire of the Sun*; they seem too personal, and I think someone will notice if I steal them. I slash my wrist and hop back into the time tunnel. This was how I won my first Booker Prize.

I enact similar crimes across time. Ripping off famous authors and turning their prose into my own bestsellers. I'm a romantic/horror/comedy/historical prize-winning novelist. I try biography and deep-dive studies of celebrated figures, but soon realise that I'd rather travel back in time and make their stories my own. Only by acts of parasitic larceny do any of us appear original. So, I pillage the classics and pre-empt major shifts in literary style. I'm the first to use cut-up techniques after I cut up Tristan Tzara in a staged barroom fight. My literary homunculus becomes the author of its own destiny. It popularises the use of book titles that have nothing to do with the contents of the story. *Vengeance of Blood Hammer* is the heart-warming tale of a baby mountain goat that helps the survivors of a plane crash in the Andes. In *The Din of Killing Pins*, a young boy comes to terms with his emerging sexuality in a strict religious household with hilarious consequences. *The Friendly Bunny's Caterpillar Companion* deals with the lingering trauma felt by an isolated island community in the aftermath of a month-long rampage by a cannibalistic serial killer. *Dog on a Raft* is about a pensioner's search for love in the sweet twilight of their life. Later, all the homunculus' novels are adapted into films or long-running TV dramas. I transport all the loot from the book sales and film rights back to my dimension and begin amassing an extravagant property portfolio.

12
the List
book club

Words pile up on words. Different squiggles connecting to different objects and ideas. These objects and ideas flow back into the words and become entwined with them like lovers. Each word once written is impossible to contain. Their meanings multiply outside of the human mind, flowing into everything and changing them forever. There is never just the text. No metaphorical construction of reality created by language where reality itself disappears in a cloud of differing contexts. That is not right. The text is connected to and yet separate from every other object and idea that ever was or will be. A vast web of strangers. An impossible knot of meaning that we can never hope to unpick. A chair is never just a chair unless someone smashes it over your head. Any attempt to reduce words or things to their essence will fail, because we can never find that core, if indeed it even exists. God had the right idea when she reduced it all to nothing. Words were born at the first stroke of the clock; it's just we never knew they were there. It took a few experimental grunts and some frantic pointing before we found them. When we did, we found them so miraculous that we imagined we'd invented them. But the invention of language never happened. We just stumbled into the words whilst out for a walk one sunny afternoon. Fuck this, I need to sit down.

'Another slice of Cherry Bakewell, love?' The kind old lady in Velcro-fastened shoes is topping up my cup with God's own tea in the Herod's Seed Cafe.

'No, I'm fine, thank you. It was delicious, but I don't want to spoil my dinner.' I offer the nice old lady my best good boy smile and we exchange some polite words that diffuse any chance of conflict in human societies. If she had been an ape, she would have clouted me for being the God-less troublemaker I so clearly was. Because now my head is shaved at the sides and spiked up on top, held rigid by hair gel and existential indignation. She eyes me kindly but with just the hint of suspicion behind her eyes: this is just the sort of Marxist insurgent the government had warned us about. CND badges, a little red star, and a Victory to the Miners sticker on a long mac. It's at least a three-hour drive at top speed to the nearest pit, but still, we are expressing solidarity here in Chaffinch-On-The-Hill.

A few months before, Jan had arrived from Gothenburg, where he had now relocated to study psychology. He came back with a new style and fresh wisdom. 'Recycle the discarded objects of the dead,' he said. He's got the charity shop look down: tweed jacket with unfashionably wide lapels, nylon shirts, button badges with new names. The Nightingales. The Pop Group. The Fall. The patches have fucked off for now. He's got a book with pictures in it. Bright erotic pictures with a dark sexual energy. Hockney and Bacon. There are heavy concepts chucked about as we suck on cans of Löwenbräu. My still-forming brain nods but I'm fucking baffled. Alienation. Angst. Freedom. Being. Nothingness. There are books by German Nazi sympathisers and French communists, Algerian anarcho-syndicalists, Danish theologians and Russian nihilists. I'm asked to put aside my disquiet and get into the ideas, man. This is where you realise the entirety of human thought is corrupted and there is no such thing as the purity of ideas you so desperately want. So, I adapt the parts I need to fit into my ever-shifting worldview. I'm barely sixteen and I'm a fucking existentialist.

'What you reading there?' The book is *Phenomenology of Perception* by Maurice Merleau-Ponty. I have absolutely no idea what it's about or what it means; it's just a jumble of words that I'm told are cool. I've glanced through it, but my mind has never settled on the contents. I just thought it would make me look interesting. I've got a pile of similar titles at home, the ones I hastily pick up when my mum comes in to tell me about my grandfather's latest operation. I tut and screw up my brow. This is angst, can't you see? To live is to suffer. We are all strapped to the hospital bed of life, mum. When she's gone I pick up the *NME* and try to memorise some acerbic Mark E. Smith remark made to a trembling journalist. Almost no other writer has had more God-like guidance attached to his work than Mark E. Smith. The Fall were my second year zero pop group. Brother Jan had primed me, but they were still just a vague concept until a holiday break with Dizzi in Devon.

We had sucked the life out of the Home Counties. Almost anyone of interest in the locality had been vampirised and left as desiccated husks. The seaside would provide new horizons and fresh victims. Dizzi had a pair of blue brothel creeper shoes which he wore with a great coat and a Cramps T-shirt. I had mid-length hair initially modelled on Alex Lifeson, but now with a slight hint of Tom Verlaine. Things were changing fast. The promise of love and peace and flowers had withered and some of my homunculi had perished in the punk rock wars or had returned to the source horribly disfigured. I no longer sought out beauty; I wanted jagged hate and world-weary absurdism.

Dizzi and I are sat around a camp fire on a Devonshire beach with a selection of the nation's youth, some from the city others from the shires. They have a variety of hairstyles and bear the insignia of their various tribes. Bauhaus, The Sisters of Mercy, Throbbing Gristle, On-U Sound, The Stooges, MC5,

The Kinks, The Action, Bhundu Boys, Blind Lemon Jefferson. I still have a sizeable bag of Seedy Sid's stash left over from the Hawkwind gig, so we are generously sharing the prescription out amongst our new friends. The gear loosens tongues.

Devonshire Beach Mixtape

Side One

1. (Love is Like a) Ramblin' Rose – Ted Taylor

2. India – The Psychedelic Furs

3. Poptones – PIL

4. She's Got Everything – The Kinks

5. Garbageman – The Cramps

6. Terror Couple Kill Colonel – Bauhaus

7. Sunny Ti De Ariya – King Sunny Adé

8. Iron Bar Dub – Linton Kwesi Johnson

9. Sham Shack – Ut

10. Hedonist Hat – Pigbros

11. Weed Seed Seed – Flashy B

12. Another Side to Mrs Quill – Yeah Yeah Noh

13. The Belldog – Eno, Moebius, Roedelius

Side Two

1. Rowche Rumble – The Fall

2. Tempa – Anthony Red Rose

3. *Adrenochrome – The Sisters of Mercy*
4. *Glimpses – The Yardbirds*
5. *Blitzkreig Bop – Ramones*
6. *Fantastic Day – Haircut 100*
7. *Making Plans for Nigel – XTC*
8. *Willow Tree – The Tremeloes*
9. *Touch of Evil – Henry Mancini*
10. *When the Night Falls – The Eyes*
11. *C'mon Everybody – UFO*
12. *Star Warz Rapso – Brother Resistance*
13. *Lord of the Hornets – Robert Calvert*

The sun was creaking above the horizon as rushing waves propelled the conversation. The different tribes had different stories. Origin tales. Myths. Different gods. Dizzi and I shared the legend of Tubs Marin, the undefeated *Defender* champion, and their mysterious presence lingering by the fruit and veg stalls of Slough's indoor market. The different tribes hooted their appreciation as we in turn saluted their own heroic tales. I exchanged a furtive glance with Dizzi. He nodded his understanding. I produced a small bag of the special red powder and held it up to the weak sunlight shafts that were beginning to encroach on our camp. 'Night cap anyone?' Eager hands shot out, nestling thumb on forefinger to receive their dose. I carefully heaped the powder in the cleft. Dizzi paused. The others sniffed. Dizzi blew the dust into the breeze. The others gawped at him. The realisation came too late, and down they went. Dizzi and I opened fresh cans of Kestrel and enjoyed the sunrise. It had been a marvellously refreshing break. If Dizzi's parents were up and about they'd be wondering where we were, so we better get back. We deployed our vampire suckers and absorbed all the cultural information we could carry in our bulging sacks. The previously lively selection of the nation's youth were now no more than morbid piles of dust. The wind picked up, sweeping in like a cleansing vapour from the ocean. Our victims mingled with the sand as the wind carried the particles inland to be dropped over cities and county towns. Dizzi and I made our way back to the cottage.

Devonshire market towns often have indoor markets where the surplus of overconsumption sits next to the dead's lifetime accumulation of artefacts. Old suits. Old suitcases. Historical fiction. Tea sets partly chipped where the dead's lips once rested. Records.

I'm digging hard through a battered box with a mental catalogue gleaned from brother Jan and the sucked-out energies of murdered youths. Flick, flick, flick. Ach, these are all crap, easy listening, military orchestras covering pop hits, big band war stuff. Suddenly I catch a white flash. A dirty, grimy white flash with a black scrawl carelessly dumped on the surface. *Totale's Turns (It's Now or Never)*. *'Are you still doing the same thing you were doing ten years ago? Well don't make a career out of it.'* Bang fucking bang the mighty Fall. Back in the cottage we annex the ancient stereo that the cottage owners have foolishly left for the use of their guests. It takes less than three minutes before the first complaint. Fuck off, man, I'm Fiery Jack from the burning ring. The first complainant is dispatched with fire. Without bothering to douse the flames of the smouldering neighbour, Dizzi and I get back into it. *'This is a groovy number.'* Songs about Swiss pharmaceutical companies, cigs, Cary Grant's nuptials, songs about Prestwich, songs about borrowed record collections, songs about Joseph McCarthy, songs about Methodist bishops, songs about muscle relaxant. This is yet another re-genesis for me. I file away the cosmic shit. For now, at least. I'll cut my hair. I'll take in my jeans and spit venom at the new puritans. I'm taking the atonal sputtered speed rap to heart. I'm going to get the fucking lot: bootlegs, demo tapes, every 7-inch, every LP, everything, even if I never buy another school meal again. I'll do the paper rounds of a thousand kids, wash every car in the county, shop lift and flog the contents of Seedy Sid's stash.

With the expansion of my collection came new titles for the psychic library, channelled directly from the grooves of The Fall's records. Nabokov, Ursula Le Guin, Colin Wilson, Lovecraft, Camus, Philip K. Dick, M.R. James. But now the words are starting to stick. I get through *Bend Sinister* in one sitting, I'm mainlining sci-fi and horror straight into my veins, real existential shit beamed into the cortex. Mark E. Smith makes pretention digestible. It's smart, tight, but rooted. I'm beginning to actually get it, man.

'I will have another slice, thanks Janet, and a top on the tea for my friend, if you don't mind.' Sometime later and I'm back in Herod's Seed Cafe. God's brew is going down well with God. She's joined me for a catch-up. Janet, that's the name of the nice old lady, who I'm glad to say I can now count as one of my friends. Janet smiles and looks somewhat starstruck. It's not every day God pops into your gift shop for a brew. Janet fills God's cup with a shaky hand. 'I'll be right back with your cake, Jonah.' Janet returns with a slice of cake and a small pile of various testaments which she nervously asks God to sign.

'With pleasure, Janet, with pleasure. And can I say you have a really lovely establishment here. You should be proud, though pride be a sin.' God's hands dance over the endpapers, adding her enigmatic sign to the testaments. Janet beams and returns to the counter clutching her signed books to her chest. God gives a cheery wave to the other assistant who is staring in disbelief at their celebrity customer. God then fixes me with a penetrating stare and an enigmatic smile. 'So, Jonah. Things are going well, I see. Congratulations on the Booker Prize by the way.'

I lean back in my chair and thrust my legs out into the room, crossing them nonchalantly.

'That's nothing, dear God. I scored the Nobel Prize last week, nobbled Marquez while he was surfing and got William Golding with a hive of trained hornets. Sucked all their stories right of them. Got my eye on Pinter next.'

'Oh, you're thinking of branching out into drama then?'

'Yeah, why not? It's all we've got, stories. Why not tell them? Any format will do: paint, prose, poems, pop. It's all nourishment. Like this delightfully light cake.'

God looked up with a guilty smile and crumbs on her lip. 'Well, I'm definitely sparing the Herod's Seed Cafe come the great flood,' she said, all the while chewing on a delicate crust.

'You've decided on the great flood, eh?' I said to her. 'Can't beat the classics.'

'I've yet to settle on the vehicle of destruction, Jonah,' she said, 'but of course I may yet spare you all. Depends on the evidence, really. Whatever evidence is. Oh, look, here's Janet with the cheque. Jonah, would you be a dear? I'm afraid I've come out without my wallet again.'

God never had her wallet. I sighed. I always had to pay the price. I picked out some money and placed it on the little silver plate Janet had put on the table. 'Thank you, Janet. Excellent as always.' I chucked in some extra coins as I thanked her. Janet smiled and was about to return to the counter when she paused and turned with a question hanging from her lips.

'Jonah, I meant to ask how you were getting on with all that time travel business?'

I looked up, mildly surprised that she had remembered my occupation. 'Oh, you know how it is,' I said to her. 'Still slicing and drifting, Janet. Still slicing and drifting.'

13

the busiest bus route in Europe

Andy Madhatter cuts in the intro of 'Unhooked Generation' by Freda Payne over looping go-go drums. Dizzi and I are on the stage blowing whistles with Elvis Lidl, the heir to the supermarket empire. Elvis is new. Elvis is a living channel to new sounds. For those readers who demand fulsome character details, he looked exactly as you imagined he would. A second-year French student with experience in the nightclub dimension. I met him on my first night in a new town. We were both fresh arrivals in Fallowfield, once a village but now a suburb, lying on the busiest bus route in Europe. We bonded over hats. I was wearing my stolen Phrygian cap; Elvis was sporting a red beret covered in 'Boy' badges. Then it was back to his for records and Breaker lager until the cock crowed. He recently inducted me into his order. Dizzi and I have, in turn, issued Elvis with vampire suckers and invited him to feed. We are all wearing the insignia of our new alliance: MA1 flight jackets and rolled up jeans. We are sucking in the vibrations of the gathered mass. It could be the Venue, The Boardwalk, The PSV, Precinct13, Konspiracy or a repurposed warehouse under the railway tracks. The heat in the room is soothing, like Satan's own living room. The Devil's pushed back the furniture and all hell is dancing. The Voices of East Harlem somehow segues into 'IMINXTC' by Denise Motto. The means of propulsion are hidden in arcane DJ practice. I want it. I want to propel records into each other just like that. I want to make the whistle blow. Elvis tells me it's possible, but there will be blood.

Mixtape for Elvis Lidl

Side One

1. *The Word/Sardines – Junkyard Band*
2. *Coast to Coast – Word of Mouth*
3. *Who the Cap Fit – Shinehead*
5. *Time to Jack – Chip E*
4. *Pump That Bass – Original Concept*

5. Triple M Bass – Worse 'Em

6. Jack Me Frankie – House People

7. Just Give the DJ a Break – Dynamix 2

8. (You Are My) All and All – Joyce Sims

9. Acid – Ray Barretto

10. White Knight Jacks – White Knight

11. Let's Get Small – Trouble Funk

12. Rock the House Part 1 – Mr K & Special G

13. Raw to Core -Mc Buzz B

Side Two

1. Deeper – Le Pamplemousse

2. I Ain't into That – The Rappin' Reverend

3. Slaughterhouse – The Funky Ginger

4. Top Billin' – Audio Two

5. The Motorcade Sped On – Steinski & The Mass Media

6. Let's Dance – Grand Groove

7. Turn Off the Lights – Larry Young's Fuel

8. Set it Off – Harlequin 4's

9. Baby's on Fire – Marc Riley and The Creepers

10. Say You – Colourbox

11. l' Elephant – Tom Tom Club

12. R-Trax – Knight Action

13. Living on the Ceiling – Blancmange

'I think you should really ask for your dad's advice on this, Jonah. I haven't got a clue. I mean, I'd say go with what you feel, like which spot has got the most clubs or bands per square inch.'

God is flicking through a prospectus for a higher education establishment. There is a pile of similar brochures scattered about on the floor of the Herod's Seed Cafe. Janet is trying to do her job, serving tea and cakes whilst stepping around our clutter. I've listened to advisors and teachers and the word of God, but I've still not made my mind up. I know what I want, but I'm torn between duty and desire.

'My dad will be no help. He wants me to be an electrical engineer like him, but I can't even change a fucking lightbulb. Plus, the fact is, I gave up physics in the fourth year but haven't had the heart to tell him yet.'

God sighs and prods me with a rolled-up prospectus. 'Not that dad, your real father, the fallen demiurge of legend, the morning star, the emperor of Babylon and master of mischief and ruin.'

'What, Santo?' I ask.

'Yes, Santo, the one who made you.'

I was adopted. We all were. I'd never met my real father, the father of us all. The Lord of the Earth. He'd dumped the lot of us at the earliest opportunity. Couldn't take the pressure of bringing up children. Feckless twot. He'd run off and joined a utopian community in Pembrokeshire called 'The Community of the Merry Spirit'. Last I heard he'd undone every attempt at peaceful consensus within the settlement with his subtle ego. It had been the same in heaven. He never could take responsibility for anything. He thought he was special and thus deserving of special treatment. No drudgery or burdensome tasks for Satan. He'd left us to bring up ourselves and what a fucking mess that had turned out to be. But maybe he could do something to help me now. Maybe on the brink of adulthood he could offer some guidance, even if it was just to avoid making the same mistakes as him. Surely he owed me that much. I kind of wanted to meet him anyway. You know, look him in the eye.

'Ok. I guess. I mean all opinions are welcome at this point.'

I don't sound convinced. I'd got so far without any fiendish pacts, not counting my deal with God of course, so why sell my soul now just for a bit of career advice? But my soul had already been sold. When I popped out in the corridor of Chaffinch-On-The-Hill maternity ward it was immediately forfeit. So, it was time to face my origin, go back to the source and meet the demon creator. It was time to summon the devil from the sulphurous pit.

God made a call on her phone. There was a bit of back and forth. A few terse whispers. God's face rippled with differing signs of frustration, but it eventually settled into something resembling acceptance. Yes. Yeah. No. Of course not. Not if you don't want to. Yes, he's here now. OK, see you in a bit. The bell above the cafe door ding-donged and Satan walked into the Herod's Seed Cafe. Janet took it surprisingly well; this good-for-nothing absentee father of all Earthly things was worse than all the members of the Chaffinch Rucking Machine deciding to plot up in your gaff. But old Christian ladies are polite. She pulled up a chair and offered him tea and cake. Satan accepted a slice of lemon drizzle and a pot of Darjeeling. I sat in my chair and exhaled with all the force of fear and frustration that I had stored up in my body. I was a late teen existentialist with a collection of space rock, post-punk, dub records and an ear for machines. I wanted out of the semi-rural straitjacket. I wanted the city lights and the dirt of Lucifer's Earthly kingdom. Santo stirred sugar into his brew. Philistine. Lucifer was a disappointment visually. I had expected a kind of beautiful golden angel like the one Milton had described in *Paradise Lost*, but he looked more like a clueless hipster who'd seen all the outfits on Instagram but couldn't quite put it all together. He'd amalgamated some of the worst features of historical fashion into an ensemble of astonishingly poor taste. Brogues, yeah, but pointy and coloured gold. Denim jeans, OK selvedge, but tight, skin tight, rolled up, no socks. Garish Hawaiian shirt depicting Hieronymus Bosch scenes open over a T-shirt with the words 'Holidays in Mordor' in hilarious spoof vacation graphics. He had a VW car logo dangling from a gold-plated chain. One was led to believe he'd stolen it from the grill of a Passat, but it was clearly from an online B-Boy catalogue. Round his neck above the chain he wore a massive Tudor ruff. He had a brocade ringmaster's tailcoat draped over his shoulders. His hair was shaved close at the sides, his fringe drooped in a wet-look kiss curl. At the back it hung down mullet style. Naturally. Baseball cap. Von Dutch. Back. To. Front. He had big fucking mirror shades on.

'What gives, my dude,' he drawled, trying to give me a handshake of staggering complexity. As I reached out my hand, he pulled his away suddenly and made to cock a snook. I could not hate him more. I paused and took him in. His head was just there, unremarkable, indescribably ordinary in a way that crushes all attempts to categorise it. If he wasn't dressed in such notably ugly clothes you would never notice him at all. That was Lucifer's trick, anonymity. He could slip in and out and you'd never know until it was too late. The mythical everyman, the homogenous unit. Satan wasn't a glorious fallen angel at all, he was a workaday nobody. So why the outfit? I suddenly realised he was dressed like this for my benefit. He was trying to relate to me. To break the ice. Like my human flesh father tapping his fingers on the steering wheel to 'Whole Lotta Love' when we drove to the Berni Inn for the Sunday carvery. I felt quite sorry for Santo, now I'd seen him up close. But that was his way too. That's how he'd subverted the good people of the 'The Community of the Merry Spirit'; he'd taken away their hope by disappointing them at every turn. There's nothing like being constantly let down to dampen the revolutionary spirit. We were all the children of this

Demon God and his imperfection permeated every one of us, but so too did that subtle ego.

×

'Objection! Objection! Satan is not on trial here. Nor has the paternity of humanity been proven. This is all hearsay and idol conjecture. How can we permit the defence to besmirch the reputation of a respected member of the demonic community by claiming, as they do, that Satan is the profligate progenitor of our species, a promiscuous, thoughtless fornicator who has wilfully abandoned his children to the types of sin and degradation the defendant has already   happily confessed to?'

The prosecutor is on his feet again. He is thumping the huge pile of evidence on his desk. The judge is taking glugs from a pewter hip flask. He is wildly drunk. The judge attempts to bang the gavel. He misses, upending an ashtray full of cigarette ends. The judge attempts to focus on the prosecutor. 'I'll allow anything at this point,' he groans.

×

Of all the 'isms' on offer to those ideologically inclined, humanism is perhaps the most misguided. It underpins them all. Faith in humanity. Because make no mistake, it is a religion like any other. The millenarian belief that, through violence, economics or the providence of history, humanity could be saved. That it would flourish and claim dominion over the world just like Satan had done after the fall. Santo, the great deceiver. The appeal to be 'more humane' as a mark of virtue was his greatest lie. Because we are the great deceivers too. Impatient and dishonest, like kids demanding ice cream before the potatoes have been finished, we want it all now. We believe we are deserving of every luxury. Every vein, root and grain are a resource to be marshalled for our God-given right to be eternally happy. But God gave us no such right. God gave us nothing. We are the children of Santo. The vain, selfish, petulant, rapacious monster plague on the face of the Earth. We don't even have the faintest idea what happiness is.

Calm down, Jonah. For God's sake. It can't be that bad. Well, no, I hope not anyway. Even pathogens can be good for you. Take those yogurt drinks you have for breakfast, the ones with the friendly bacteria. We could be like that. Tasty and nutritious as part of a balanced diet. Evolution is not progress, because there is no such thing as progress. But evolution is change. We can change. It is not about going back or reconnecting with some great lost wisdom, because we were never wise. It's about becoming something new. A possible benign mutation. That particular insight was what Santo stole from the good people of 'The Community of the Merry Spirit'; he made them believe they were already gods, that they were already the measure of all things. So, when the realities of power, of psychic violence, domination, greed and prejudice bit into their communal oneness, the shock froze them all in a terrifying stasis. Santo kept them rooted, unable to move, perpetually repeating the same mistakes again and again, but with different names. Every change in science, society, culture or politics came with its own dark passenger. A consensus for cruelty, despots with mandates, a calculus of worth where those that did not make the grade were dispatched for the good of the whole, cheap power with fallout, cheap clothes with poison, happy meals with a billion ground-up hooves. This was what the children of Santo had made. But still we had faith. Faith in the right of man. Humanism is the worst sort of 'isms'. Let's do away with 'isms' of all kinds, let's just jump in and jive, with all the filth and horror and all the light and shade that entails. In the sweat-drenched basement when the kick drum pounds and the energy of all the gathered human souls morph into one big ball of ego death. When I am you and me is we and we are all together. In the strobe light's flashing morse code, that is where possible salvation lies. In the acceptance of drums.

'The head of department at Hull is supposed to be a leading authority on the ontology of the Austrian Postal service.' Satan is helping me with my UCCA form, but I can't help thinking he's missing the point. Brix has joined The Fall and they are in the process of releasing a peerless run of records: *Perverted by Language, The Wonderful and*

Frightening World, *This Nation's Saving Grace*, *Bend Sinister*, *The Frenz Experiment* and *I Am Kurious Oranj*. Brix injects fresh impetus into their post-garage punk growl, directing them out of the lo-fi cul de sac and pushing them out into the sun. It's exhilarating, acerbic, heavy duty psych pop that sounds like the future and the past simultaneously. Further doors are opened. I'm at the theatre watching *Hey! Luciani*, getting into avant-garde ballet and Michael Clark, who as it turns out was trained by my great uncle Len, former dancer at the Royal Ballet and close friend of Margot Fonteyn. I'm almost a fully grown sophisticate trapped in a metro land stockade. The Fall are my accomplices in the great break-out. I attend every gig I can. I'm up front, sucking in the energy of Prestwich and its environs. At home there is a north-western geographical slant to my record collection, every other album originates in one place. Manchester.

'You need a vocational course, something to set you up with a decent career. Business studies maybe, or if it has to be the arts, how about psychology? The world is going to need a lot of psychologists. Sports science, physiotherapy, politics.' Santo glances up from the prospectus and looks me up and down from over the rims of his shit shades. Fuck this guy, trying to get the measure of me with one glance. 'Perhaps nothing too sporty,' he says. 'I like the look of Brighton for economics, or Keele for agricultural management ...'

'Fuck that, Santo.'

Then God cuts in. 'Can't you see the boy's made up his mind?' she says. Satan is put out. He looks at me. I shrug and take a bite from my cake. Satan purses his lips. 'I think I know my own son, thank you,' he says.

But God shakes her head and slowly raises her hand. Suddenly, everything is silent. Shoppers put down birthday cards. Shop assistants lay down their scented candles. Janet puts down her tray of tea cups. All eyes turn to God. Then God's voice booms out with all its familiar harmonious authority: 'Manchester, to study philosophy and the impending youth culture explosion. It's all totally useless in every way possible, and thus perfect. The time for useful things is at an end. I have spoken. And will hear no more on the subject. Get packing, Jonah, it's time to hit the north.'

The journey was long. Manchester is further north than I had imagined, and my mother's Vauxhall Chevette was struggling up the M1 laden down with my records and magical paraphernalia. With every clunking kilometre it became apparent that I was not as worldly wise as I had imagined. The world outside the windscreen was alien and mythical. These were places I had read about in newspapers or had only seen on the TV. Places where Margaret Thatcher's war on society was being fought. The front line in some hideous misreading of Darwin, where the fittest were forgotten, discarded and left to decay, while the short-term thinking of supine clowns were exulted. I was getting on my bike just like Norman Tebbit suggested, but I was in search of communal ecstasy and teenage kicks. Through the wastelands of free market claptrap, into the Cheshire fields, the Vauxhall Chevette puffed and strained until we reached the outskirts of the nuclear-free utopia of Greater Manchester. It was a scarred landscape of neglected glory, but even through the flyblown windscreen it was obviously alive. Posters. Fucking posters everywhere announcing a million cultural happenings. Kids in weird uniforms. Androgenous energies and punk-rock militants. Anarchists on buses with record shop bags. Haircuts of varying degrees of complexity. A living, breathing fuck-you to the headlines of inner-city decline. A shit hole with soul, man. My mum dropped me off at my new home. She was sad. Her only child flown the nest with all his magical instruments. I was sad too, I guess. Sad because she was. But really I was out the door as soon as the Vauxhall's taillights were out of sight. Still, metro land invaders need to earn their stripes. This ain't Chaffinch-On-The-Hill, young man. No time for gawking tourism or make-believe solidarity with a world you never knew existed. You need to be born again, young Jonah. You need some sense punching into you, you daft wanker.

I'm in Rusholme Chippy. Elvis and I have been out on the town. He's stumbled ahead into the Fallowfield hinterlands. But I need salt and starch fried to perfection. 'Salt and vinegar?' I nod, my head lolling from side to side in a drunken roll. I'm wearing Attis's Phrygian cap, the loon pants from 1969, a denim cut-off from the Hollister riots, a long mac with a Bauhaus button badge and a Bones Brigade T-shirt in lurid pink. I'm a fashion mess but comfortable with my choices. 'You want gravy with that, kidda?' The chip chef is holding the paper cone open and fixing me with a quizzical eye and a raised eyebrow. I pause. My drunken wobble suddenly steadies as I sense a puzzle. Gravy? On chips?! This is not something that is possible. It is like ice in a desert or a living lamb in a wolf's den. This must be a trick. A friendly joke at my expense. That famous northern humour I've heard all about. Up until this moment I have not uttered more than a slurred murmur to accompany some pointing, but now my voice rings out like Horatio Hornblower on sighting a French frigate: 'Gravy?! Dear God, man, what do you take me for?' There is a momentary pause in the movement of the universe. Time stops. All motion ceases. Even the subatomic dance of particles is brought to a temporary standstill. A man who, up until that moment, I had been unaware even existed is also frozen in time. His mouth caught between shock and fury. Don't ask me to describe him, dearest reader, as it would be a fruitless fiction; just imagine he is an avatar for alienated labour, the embodiment of a Friday night out after a shit week in a shit job. Just a normal bloke trying to get by until the end of the month who has stopped off for a late-night snack from a reliable local food outlet. Imagine he is a patronising caricature dreamt up by a disconnected middle-class author from another time and place who has never done a decent day's work in his fucking life, and who is now struggling to describe an assailant in a fictional historical account of his life in Manchester in the late 1980s. Now imagine he is staring at the multicoloured, insanely attired, distillation of privilege and the north/south divide. Slowly. Very slowly, like a slug cruising across a leaf, I try to smile, having only just realised my error. Too late. Thwack! The stranger is released from his spell. That's for Peterloo, you southern ponce. Thwack! Thwack! That's for monetarism and trickle-down economics. Kick! Thwack kick! He's a lively one. I'm reminded of Michael Clark's routine in the 'Lay of the Land' video. This fellow is nimble and accurate, just like Michael. I wonder if he knows my great uncle Len? Thwack! Slap! Kick! He makes the subtlest of pirouettes as he scoops up the pile of chips from the chip chef and rubs them into my Phrygian cap. He adds his saliva to the chip fat and leaves the takeaway without giving me another thought. It's good to get closure, I think to myself. The chip chef is looking down at me from the counter. 'Curry sauce, perhaps?' the chip chef offers helpfully. I'm fucking *in*, man. This is my town now.

The sandpit is now like a dimensionless desert. There is no visible horizon. Just the odd somnolent head nodding in the breeze. A dry wind hacks and harries the sand, whipping it up into tiny tornadoes that spit dust in the faces of the happy, sleepy heads. I tut and clean the grit off a new 7-inch single that I got free from the cover of the *NME*. It's a four-track EP with some crackers on it: Elvis Costello, Billy Bragg and Miles Davis. Their heads are already sticking out of the sand of the laboratory. But it's the fourth number that really pricks up the ears. 'Hardcore Hip Hop' by Mantronix. It's the sound of vinyl being cut to ribbons over the heaviest, craziest MPC drum machine workout ever conjured. Over the top of the thumping beats, MC Tee extols the virtues of Kurtis Mantronik's production techniques and the combined effectiveness of rhyme and rhythm. It's fascinating. Like the mutated offspring of Jamaican dancehall and New York funk as played by frustrated cyborgs. This is the sound of a firing squad putting one in the chamber and taking aim at the bloated rock and roll monster. Dizzi struggles across the sand dragging a sack.

'Word up, Dizzi,' I say, using the newly discovered hip hop vernacular.

'Peace,' he replies, dumping the sack in front of me. Something is struggling inside.

'What you got there?' I ask him.

'Fresh victims, my friend,' he says, loosening the string around the sack. A man tumbles out, catching his breath and blinking in the desert sun. He looks up at Dizzi and me and smiles.

'Hey, I'm Kurtis Mantronik,' he says.

'Hi, pleased to meet you,' we chorus.

'You must be tired after being dragged across the desert like that. Why don't you rest and take some refreshment,' I say to him, indicating a comfortable, freshly dug hole.

'That hole certainly looks comfortable. Shady too. Do you mind if I climb in?' he says.

'Why, of course, be our guest.'

Kurtis pops into the hole and we tidy the loose sand around him until only his head is showing above the ground.

'There you are, nice and cosy. Now let me get you something to drink,' I say. Dizzi chats to our new guest, who seems very happy in the cool sand, while I fix up the potion. 'Here you go,' I say, while placing the straw into Kurtis Mantronik's parched mouth. 'I think you will find this very relaxing.' He gives the straw a good suck.

'Oh, thank you, yes, that is a delightful cordial, very unusual taste. Familiar, though I can't quite place it.' His eyelids are already beginning to droop. Within moments he is happily sedated. Dizzi and I deploy our vampire suckers and begin to feed.

1986: young people in the capital are living in the 1970s, wearing flares, fancy waistcoats, doing the rowing dance and listening to 'Oops Upside Your Head'. This is the cutting edge of fashionable club culture for some. I'm a time traveller, so this is all cool with me, but time travellers like to go forward as well as back, so here in my new home, in Manchester, I've found the rumblings of a musical revolution punctuating the retro funk. A fresh musical backbone. A strong foundation built from a new man/machine hybrid. House music. Elvis Lidl, Dizzi and I are about to be changed beyond recognition. We've done the rounds of the sub-goth/indie watering holes. We've had the good funk, Latin, rare soul sound with Dean and John Tracey. Fizz has refreshed us hip hop wise in the Man Alive. The PSV is essential. The Gallery is alive with the peerless sounds of Hewan Clarke. The city is alive. Mike Shaft. The Jam MCs. Owen D. Leaky Fresh. Sefton Terminator. Stu Allen. Buss Diss. Times are nice in the post-industrial heartlands. These are foundation sounds. But at every dance, in every club, every DJ in town is peppering their sets with an insistent mantra. A sound that causes the whistle posse to blow like Albert Ayler. Time to Jack. Time to jjjjack the house. I'm in a converted yacht builder's warehouse on Whitworth Street. What the fuck a yacht builder was doing by Rochdale canal is a mystery. The space has been repurposed into an entertainment venue, designed in an impeccable modernist style, given an oblique situationist name and sent out into the world to blow minds. Elvis has taken me there as a part of my initiation rite. It's Friday. The night is called Nude. The disc jockeys are Martin Prendergast and Mike Pickering. Two local lads with divine knowledge. Elvis leads me in through these weird butcher's curtains that are draped over the entrance to the club. Inside, the gaff looks like all my fantasies of urban sophistication made flesh. If only Janet and the ladies of Herod's Seed Cafe could see me now. But the appreciation of design is not what grabs my attention. It's the sound. The space is post-industrial, a ludic temple reclaimed from the waste of economic decline. So is the sound. This is post-capitalist rhumba. Products meant to sedate the populace and keep them from rising up have been converted into weapons. Musical devices kidnapped and coaxed into countercultural activities. The sound bounces out of the speaker stacks in scattergun waves, insinuating itself into the bricks until the whole building feels like one great acid lung. Breathing in and out. It's relentless, freeform, hypnotic machine hymnals. Meaningless, nihilistic, structureless, endless. And in that meaninglessness, the total essence of life. The dissolution of form into feeling. A pulse to match the beating of your heart. The sparse words, where there are any at all, are simple poems that carry more weight than any political polemic or protest song. It's time to jack. We've got to come together. Someday we'll all be free. HHH-HHousenation. This is the revolution right fucking here. No manifesto required. Elvis is talking to a dude wearing flares, sporting a perfect bowl haircut and Clarks shoes. Around them the joint is jumping. The Foot Patrol pull off impossible dance moves in smart jazzer suits and spats. Whistles. Everywhere there is the sweet sound of whistles. Elvis and the bowl-haired dude whisper into each other's ears. Heads nod. Smiles break out. Hands flash as goods are exchanged. Elvis returns with the holy sacrament. The initiation is nearly complete. Elvis hands me a pill. He grins at me as he chucks one down his throat and chases it with a raspberry seltzer. Fuck it. I follow his example and throw mine down too. As if the music hadn't been enough. I mutate and become something new. It's 7am in some stranger's flat in Hulme. I'm no longer an existentialist. I'm a fucking evangelist.

14

Love

I love everybody. I don't mean I desire everybody. Though that is also true, I mean I love everybody. I want to be everybody and have them, in turn, be me. Because there is no longer any such thing as me or them, there is only we. An amazing, fuzzy oneness. A kick in the eye for Thatcherite individualism and the selfish 1980s. There is no retreat behind the doors of gated communities or sold-off council housing stock. We won't be told there is no such thing as society. We've got machines and love drugs; we've got Byron Stingily, Elkin and Nelson. It's nothing like punk: this is no art school nihilist's situationist prank; this is the expression of collective joy. Tear down the walls, motherfuckers, liberation is at hand! When that first chemical bond was forged in the mess of my brain, in the spongy trampoline of memory and thought, I fell in deep, deepest love with all my fellow beings, human, animal and mineral. Drugs are great.

Acid house is great. Everything else can just fade away. That was my new ideal. In the smoke of the machine's breath, while the strobe strobed and the kick drum thumped, when the raspberry seltzer went down and the ecstasy merged with my blood, in that moment I was born again. Woosh. I love the gangster dude with the craggy face, I love mushroom head, I love Pam Hogg leggings girl, I love Moon and Baz the hat, I love Johnny Acid and Everyday Steve, I love kicking ambient and Posh Mitherer, I love Jilly Jingles and the Wigan Away Team, I love Emma Two Shoes and Rebecca's Cigarettes. I love Elton's hat and the bit under it, I love Steve the Mooch and Johnny Leather Pants. I fucking love Ten City.

Can a demon love? Can I love? Because I am the son of a demon god and that makes me at least part demon, surely? Is anything entirely evil? Am I evil? Is anything entirely good? Am I good? I suppose that is the underlying judgement to be made in any legal tussle. Does that one act of evil, even taken in isolation, negate any counter acts of good the defendant might have habitually indulged in. But this is surely just a matter of getting caught. The criminal is only a careless saint. The innocent saint would never dream of getting arrested. They would play a far cannier game. Take the saint who was cozy with brutal dictators. The saint who supped at the table of murderers. Do the crimes of tyrants in turn leave their stain on them? Hide the paper trail and wait for death. The canonised can endure any slander. The philanthropist with a questionable search history on their laptop. Keep it encrypted. The celebrated surgeon who fixes the needy and those displaced by war, but as a child enjoyed blow-torching ant nests. Carefully edit out that detail in the autobiography. The anti-war activist who harbours a secret racist animus towards an ancient people. Indulge in radical doublethink. The kind leader who would carpet bomb their enemies if given half a chance. Smoke. And. Mirrors. The shiny pop star. Things were different then. The inspirational teacher with a roving eye. No one believes the rumours. Nothing is pure. Not art. Not music. No saint. No god. Mistakes. Evil. Blasphemy. This is all part of the Demon God's gift. No one can opt out. Purity is an illusion and should be avoided at all costs. I'm not a bad demon. But I am as guilty as sin. We all are. But I can love. Because love isn't about the binary. Good or evil. It's just the urge to go, go, go. Satan loved attention. Satan loved respect. So, when mother was too distracted to offer either, Satan made a mess. Satan loved his mother and Satan loved his mess. That mess is us, by the way. We are the result of a crime of passion. A crime of love.

7am in some flat in Hulme. 1988. I'm with Dizzi, Elvis and The Wisdom. The Wisdom is a psych head and has found his way here by another path, but we all get it. 66, 67, 68, 88. Acid turned you on and in. E turns you on and out. We've drawn a sonic line from Terry Riley's organ, up the sleeve of King Tubby's vest, through Mancuso's loft and into the kitchen of a post-war housing experiment gone astray. We are with some nice people we met a few hours ago on a podium on Whitworth Street. We are all as high as balls. Time has ticked on. The south has finally got into house music. Some cockney chaps are handing out miniature teddy bears and smiley badges around the flat. We are all getting into a mixtape of Graeme Park from 1987: *Live from the Northern House Review*. North and south are entwined in a big puddle of love as seamless acid sounds blend into each other like impossible alchemy. All former rivalry, if there ever was any, is forgotten; we are all now one Housenation. The cockneys have come up on a coach to check out the grey wastes of northern England. They soon find its a kaleidoscope up here too. We've been jacking for years, so acid house ain't no big surprise. There are whistles blowing in the Moss every weekend from dusk till dawn. But these London cats have added a bit of cosmic spice to the soup. The new love energy and loose fit aesthetics. I'm sitting in the remains of a zoot suit while a lady from Streatham tells me about Balearic beat. I've adapted my smart club couture to fit in with this new wave of dissent. No more fancy garments; from now on it's all Converse and beads for me. The zoot suit is torn from my body in a ritual cleansing ceremony and a multicoloured poncho is lowered over Attis's Phrygian cap and on to my willing shoulders. The cap itself is then magically transformed into a tight-fitting woven prayer hat. Its versatility endures. The

South London massive gives me the thumbs up. The Mancs nod their approval as they get into Chipie and Chevignon. A huge pile of once-cherished designer clobber forms in the centre of the flat. We all dance around it, rejecting shallow materialism while sniffing amyl nitrate. It's become apparent during the evening that it's going to be a long summer of love, because that rush I'd been having for the last few months now has a message and the message is love. Ibiza is wedded to Chicago, New York, Detroit, Nottingham, Manchester, Liverpool, Glasgow, London, Bristol, even Chaffinch-On-The-Hill. The new age of Aquarius is here.

A Mixtape for the South London Massive that I Met at an Afterparty in Hulme

Side one

1. Psychedelic Jack – Extasis

2. Fallout – Pilot Jones

3. Shake Your Body – Jeanette Thomas

4. Straight Out the Jungle – Quest

5. Take Me Higher – Colm III

6. Out of Control – O.N.I.T

7. Hardcore on the One – Duane & Co.

8. Machines – Laurent X

9. Cheebala – Ghentlon

10. Don't Dub – Dean Anderson

11. Ease the Pressure – Subliminal Aurra

12. Rocket 2U Dub – The Jets

13. Spicy – G-Force

Side Two

1. Fast and Slow – M.B.

2. One Night in My Life – Akasa

3. Truth of Self Evidence – Reese

4. Ital's Theme – Ital Rockers

5. Technological – Bizarre Inc

6. Cool J Trax – House Gang

7. Metre – E.D. - 209

8. Don't Panic – Revolutionary Tactics

9. Karn Evil – Xperiment

10. Rebels – Jamie Principle

11. Muzik – Myoshi Morris

12. Here We Go – The Project

13. Art of Acid – Victor Romeo & The Move

In a warehouse just off the Oldham Road, a collective of wizards are doing some impossible shit with records. I know the sounds. Centerfield Assignment, Ghentlon, Teque Nick, Victor Romeo, Fast Eddie, Duane & Co., Phuture. But the DJs are rearranging them into one collective wave of sound. Staccato lyrics machine gun out over clattering rimshots; acid pulses hold down the trance beats. I don't know where I am, and I don't care. Everyone is together.

Everyone is moving as one. Everyone is in love with everyone else. It's not all good though; I miss the expressive jazz dancers and their sweaty spats. The dance here is far more uniform. Arms pivoting in harmony like a windmill. The expression here is not one of individual prowess on the floor, it's the will of one human organism living right here, right now. People look wide-eyed into each other's dilated pupils. The heat is intense. The DJs are hidden, almost invisible. The connections they make are not those of the strutting rock god or the angry new wave auteur, they are invisible cords leading from vinyl grooves up the cartridge and into the minds of the organism. Like all good artists, the DJ lets the record speak. This is the death of the rock star, and the triumph of the reluctant exhibitionist. I could get into this. To be able to share the sound, to officiate in this great ritual without being the centre of anything, is my idea of art. I must become like them. Steve Williams, Mike Pickering, Jon Dasilva. I only know it's them because I saw the flyer, but because I've just started working in a record shop, I know their tastes.

The record shop. Western Front Records. The most important building in the world. More powerful than the White House, the Vatican, or any parliament. It's a social hub, an information node, a dispensary serving addicts, a sacred space. This is where records rest before going out into the world. It's an incubation ward. It's a place for contemplation and a space to hear the word. I spend hours, days, years at the counter absorbing sounds and spending whatever funds I have on making them mine. The counter staff are intermediaries distributing the sacrament. Behind the counter are untidy rows of covetable artefacts. Under-the-counter precious gems. I want them. I want them all. I want to horde the treasure and roll about on a bed of records like some Tolkienesque character corrupted by gold. As academic education finishes and the accolades are allotted, so the search for work begins. In this dimension the oppressive structures of capitalism still hold sway, and I'm forced to find employment to pay for my habits. The record shop would be the perfect place to combine the two. But Western Front Records is fully staffed, and despite the frantic pace and poor wages there have so far been few casualties. I perch myself on the counter like a vulture waiting for someone to drop. Then one day the pressure on one particularly sensitive member of staff gets too much and he is sacked on the spot while I'm hovering about the check out. Never one to pass up the chance of exploiting someone's misfortune, I immediately volunteer my services and take his job. My morbid lurking has paid off. Now I am resident at the source of sound. The record shop. Western Front Records. I'm in. The treasure will soon be running through my greedy fingers. I'll steal what I can and get discount on the rest.

Back in the warehouse Steve Williams, Mike Pickering and Jon Dasilva are whipping the frequencies into new surging patterns. But I can't see them. I can only feel. There is too much smoke, too many lights, too much sound. What do we care about watching DJs when we can inhabit the waves that they create; who wants to see a nodding head when you can connect to an entire warehouse full of delicious life force. DJs are conduits. DJs are conductors. We are the stars. All of us.

Elvis flips an E across space, and I catch it in my mouth like a sealion. Dizzi is lost in a trance with his eyes closed swaying from side to side. The Wisdom is doing a mad freakout routine running around the perimeter of the dance waving his hands out in front of him like he's casting a spell. I'm lost in the sound. Future FJP is playing loud. I'm moving my fingers in time to the music like I'm tapping on cymbals. Future FJP segues into Stabbed 'You Are Mine', then this weird metallic voice starts to punctuate a new song. A vocoder telling me to turn the knob, to do a good job, to wind up on the grid.

My trance dance stops. Everyone else continues to move. If anything, the dance jumps up another notch. But I'm momentarily left out of the flow. Why? Why has my beautiful meditation been so rudely interrupted? I look for God. I look for Satan. But I'm alone. Completely isolated behind some infernal screen. Then it hits me. I don't know what the record playing is. I have spent years and almost all my money on records, I have read every available magazine and music paper, I have absorbed every chart, I work in the most prestigious and well stocked record shop in the North West of England, so how the fuck don't I know what this record is? It's an afront to all that is sacred. But it's so fucking good. My body demands I ignore the desire to break out of the dance and find out what it is. That old mind/body thing again. A truce is called as I rhythmically slide across the room in the direction of the DJ box. I'm moving, my mind is moving, we are all moving. That song. It's too fucking good. I must know it. I must possess it. On the way I hug sweaty football hooligans, office clerks, hairdressers, students and foundry operatives. I score some speed from an off-duty police officer. At last, I reach the booth, but the journey has taken days and the song has melted into something else entirely. Something on Nu Groove that I already know. Fuck. The DJ booth has a door to keep out twats like me. I bang on it. Mike Pickering answers it. A smile looks like it's exploded on his face, he's dripping with sweat, he's wearing a 'Numero Uno' T-shirt, once yellow now a kind of perspiration grey. It's hard to hear over the thud of the future, so I have to shout. 'Mike, what was that record you played a minute ago, the one that was going on about turning knobs on the grid or something?'

Jon Dasilva waves at me from behind his record box. I can see that Kraftwerk record he plays sticking out. Fuck, I love that record. I want to get back to the dance before it starts up. Now Steve Williams is playing. He's cutting up Al-Naafiysh over a Reese and Santonio number. Jesus, it's spectacular. I need to get amongst it. But that tune. *The* tune. I look at Mike Pickering with pleading eyes. What was that number, Mike. I must know – the survival of all living things depends on it.

'It's a tune on Nu Groove, Jonah,' he replies, his mouth now engaged in some form of complex acrobatics. 'Tuch Me by Da Noyz Boyz'.

'No, not that one, I know that one. Good number. But it was … the one before …'

Grinning wildly, Pickering closes the hatch, and I'm left staring at the pitted wood. My body demands we return to the podium. Just another fucking mystery. But I am a fiend, and fiends must feed. So, I return to suck on the lifeforce of the rave.

It's fuck knows o'clock on Sunday morning. The warehouse is still full, but the police have arrived and so it's time to split. The Wisdom has lost it and is making his way up the Oldham Road shouting the speech from an MC5 live album in the faces of some bemused postal workers who've just finished the night shift. 'Are you willing to testify?' he asks. One or two signal their willingness and so The Wisdom moves on down the road. Dizzi has his eye on some garage punk kids with mad deer stalker hats on; they are rocking a raw rock and roll aesthetic that's sharp and mean, but they too are full of love drugs and are high on hope. Dizzi is going to drain them good, so I leave him to it. Elvis has disappeared entirely, so I'm left alone on a twilight-speckled street still wondering what that record is. I later receive a phone call from Elvis telling me his father has sadly past away, and he has been forced to return home to assume control of the Lidl supermarket empire. He still sends me a Lidl bumper hamper every Christmas, though we no longer go clubbing together.

Fuck knows o'clock is just the time to invite friends round to your house for drinks and chat, so when I spot Jon Dasilva and Mike Pickering coming out of the warehouse hefting crates of records. I think it only polite to invite them back to my yard. I still have a reasonable amount of drugs left in my pockets, plus the residue of Seedy Sid's stash, and my wine cellar is famed in the Whalley Range and Chorlton area, so a pleasant morning is guaranteed. Mike and Jon seem glad of the invitation, so we jump into a passing taxi.

From the profits of my stolen art career and the film adaptations of my stolen novels, I have purchased an enormous Victorian house in Whalley Range. This momentarily surprises my guests, who are sceptical that a young man of barely twenty-one years working in a record shop with a degree in philosophy can afford such a palatial home. Because in this dimension that is how I appear, not as the world-famous author and artist that I am in other time streams, but as an annoying, pimply ex-student trying to break into music. However, unknown to the residents of this time and place, cash carries across the barriers, so I'm more than flush; I'm secretly minted. 'Please make yourselves at home,' I say. 'Oh, and don't mind them, they're staying with me for a while. Jon, Mike, this is ... actually I'm not sure I know their names, sorry. Anyway best ignore them, they are harmless but possibly too far gone now to make much sense.' I had forgotten that I had let the ravers out of the cellar for some exercise and here they were wandering around the living room bumping into the furniture. How embarrassing. I was hoping to impress my guests, who I admired greatly, and this sort of untidiness would not create a good impression. I attempted to herd the ravers into a controllable clump, but they were too jittery to control. This wasn't the first time my naturally inquisitive nature had got me into trouble. Of course, there was my divine mission to consider, my gnostic quest. Without data, how could I hope to show God what made us tick? On this occasion I had been keen on studying the effects of prolonged ecstasy use on the young, and so I had harvested this modest group of three in the aftermath of a particularly vigorous afterparty four or five months ago. I had kept them imprisoned in my cellar, feeding them on a diet of Es, chewing gum and Lucozade. I had made extensive notes on their progress and was pleased with the results. They were still alive, which was surprising, but had undergone quite significant physical changes. They were bald – in fact they had lost all their body hair – they glowed slightly, and they looked strangely elongated like stick insects. But they were happy. During the day I would pipe the KLF's *Chill*

Out album into the cellar, and at night I would let them run around the living room as I practised my DJ skills on my modest home set-up. I had no neighbours so we could really smash it out at times. It was fun. Anyway, here they were staring blankly at these two legends of the acid house, and I was feeling embarrassed.

'Don't worry, Jonah, they seem like a nice bunch,' Jon Dasilva said helpfully. 'Why don't you fix us some drinks and I'll stick a few tunes on.'

This was an excellent idea. I was in awe of Jon's mixing skills, and the thought of being able to watch him play in the comfort of my own living room was just too good to be true. My zombie raver captives seemed pleased too, as they began to hop up and down on their spindly stick legs. I went out to the kitchen and poured some potent cocktails as the opening bars of 'Virgo Mechanically Replayed' echoed down the corridor.

Is possession really a crime? Possession is nine-tenths of the law, as they say, so is the occupation of someone's mind and body not simply a clear case of squatters' rights? Possession, in my case at least, was rarely undertaken for coercive reasons: it wasn't malicious, but more a case of study. It wasn't that I simply found myself a quiet corner of someone's consciousness and took notes. I definitely wasn't a bystander or a witness. Because to understand someone properly, one must become that person, one must inhabit their every thought and movement, one must be them. But is that a crime? No one got hurt. Well, occasionally, and I'm happy to plead guilty to those incidents, but generally speaking, that wasn't the case. If I may refer to the case of the possession of Jon Dasilva as a perfect example, whereby the act of possession no way inconvenienced the possessed as they were completely unaware of the intrusion. No changes were made to the possessed, neither physically or mentally, no damage was done to reputation or financial wellbeing. In fact, possession could well claim to have been a great benefit to humanity, as it led to Jonah Plantagenet becoming the worlds most celebrated disc jockey and remixer. The world would, I think you'll agree, be a whole lot less joyful without Plantagenet's work with the resurrected Beatles or his universally lauded hologram world tour, not to mention his inspirational set on the roof of Buckingham Palace in honour of the crowning of the new emperor. His clever mash-ups of world leaders' speeches throughout history woven over a relentless trance beat, beamed into every home on the planet. That was history. But, without that tiny initial act of possession, none of those glorious moments would have occurred. Surely, in this case, the ends clearly justify the means.

In the late 1980s all DJs drank vodka and orange. It was a kind of mandatory sacrament. This was, by happy coincidence, the perfect drink with which to possess some-one. Due to its overpowering tartness, it's easy to mix almost anything in with it and still avoid detection. While

Jon spun tunes in the living room and the zombie ravers hopped about, I cut the top of my index finger off, stuck it in a blender with some ice, orange juice and a generous glug of Kommissar vodka and created a refreshing screwdriver. I decanted the contents into a serving jug and placed it on a tray with my best tumblers. I still had a reasonable amount of Seedy Sid's gear that I had stolen from him at the Slough Fulcrum Hawkwind gig. I kept them in a hidden panel behind the washer-dryer in the kitchen. Some Es, cocaine, admittedly not the best quality, but passable, a light dusting of speed and the bag of weird-looking, blood red powder that I thought it wise to avoid. That particular substance was reserved for acts of liquidation. There was something unholy about it. Satan's own nose bag. I returned the red powder to its secret hole. I emptied out some ecstasy tablets into a charming porcelain cup that I had picked up on my last time trip to Ming dynasty China. Using a sugar bowl as a receptacle, I then mixed cocaine and speed into a pleasing crystalline pile. A dainty silver spoon completed the tea set. I rejoined the party, which was going very well. My guests happily received my offerings. I fed the zombie ravers, who began to career around the living room with increased vigour. Inside the blood of Mike Pickering and Jon Dasilva, I began to take shape. I occupied each cell one by one. Blossoming like algae in their veins and arteries. I began to travel. Into their limbs. Into their eyes, into their minds. I could see my home through their eyes. I watched the sham-

bling zombies rebound off the sofa. I scanned my bookshelves, judging the owner's taste by the titles on display.
Their fingers – my fingers – flicked through my records. I
felt the movement of their necks as they nodded in approval
at Television or Cabaret Voltaire. I felt the swish of a head
shake and the outlet of amused breath when their fingers
came across Captain Mooneasy's cover version of Captain
Sensible. I heard the laughter ring out through their ears.
I'm in Jon Dasilva's eyes. I see the decks and the mixer. LED
levels dance up and down on the channels. The records are
spinning. I see pitch control and the tracer of dots on the
turntable platter. I feel the subtle touch as his fingers deftly
slow or speed up the disc. Thud. Thud. Thud. Everything is
in perfect time. With his ears I sense a growing disturbance,
not yet perceptible to those in the room. It is time travel.
Into the future. With Jon Dasilva's ears I can hear the clash
of beats yet to come. With his fingers I feel the faintest of
twists on the spindle that changes the future and brings
harmony back to the beat before any disturbance is felt.
Jon Dasilva is rinsing the groove. He is writing poetry with
machine boogie discs. Inside his eyes I'm crying. This is too
beautiful. So this is how it's done. This is how it feels. This
is art in action. Then I realise it's not a skill at all. It isn't the
imposition of form on inert matter. This isn't manipulation.
This is music talking. This is possession. Because inside Jon
Dasilva I am not alone. Music is here too, and it is music
that is moving his fingers and pumping his heart. Music

that is pushing the currents of electricity through his brain. Music singing up the needle and out of the speakers in my fucking living room. A DJ is a conductor, an interface, a conduit. The medium. I look through the record crate he has carried back from the acid house. All the records in his box are alive.

Twelve days later and Jon finally calls a taxi and heads home. The zombie raver captives have been returned to the cellar where they are getting into 'Slow Waves, Soft Stars' by Anthony Phillips. Mike is telling me about his years living in New York and the early days of Factory Records. He plays me the new T-Coy record, which is fucking amazing. I decide to clone him. I've already sucked out as much inspiration and information as I can handle with my vampire suckers. I've even found out the title of that mystery record he played in the warehouse off the Oldham Road. But there is so much more to learn from Mike Pickering, so I figure it's best for me to imprison him in my cellar with the zombie ravers and quickly clone him before I go to sleep. I'll let him out in time for Nude night. I have been awake for over a fortnight, so after tidying up a bit, I go to bed. Sleep deprivation is the enemy of efficient criminal activity. I must have forgotten to lock the shackles in my dungeon cellar, because when I get up I find the cellar door open and the zombie raver captives gone. Both Mike Pickerings have also fled. There is a note on the kitchen table.

Thanks for a great night, had a top time. Your friends seem very nice. Give us a bell later in the week. I've got a mate with a record label who you should meet. I reckon you've got a decent album in you somewhere. Not sure about the Captain Sensible cover though!

Love Mike(s)

0161 447 1423

Amazing! I've got a handwritten note from one of my DJ heroes. He's left his phone number, and he wants me to try my hand at making some music. He didn't seem too concerned about the imprisonment or the cloning either, so all's well that ends well, I guess. This was how Jonah Plantagenet's meteoric rise to fame began. Was this a crime? Surely not? A little unorthodox perhaps, but everyone got out alive. I even heard that the cloned Mike Pickering went on to have a very successful recording career with M-People.

15

Pat Gloom and the Court of King John

Can I get a witness? I'm not appealing for endorsements here. I'm not looking for validation by a third party. I'm not looking for experts, doctors, clinical psychologists or micro forensic scientists. I don't need their testimony. I'm not striving for leniency from the court on grounds of diminished responsibility. I don't need the voices of others to prove the validity of my confession. God is my witness on that account. No, I want a witness to show the court that my crimes, if you can call them that, were simply acts of love. I want to hear from friends and allies, from fellow enthusiasts, from admirers, and from those who despise me too. I want them to testify with hands on the sacred book. Their hands on a tatty copy of *Son of a Demon God* that now stands as *the* text on which every consecrated oath must be taken. In every courtroom in every part of the world the confessions of Jonah Plantagenet have taken on a sacral quality that unifies both the innocent and the guilty. No one would dare to lie once their hand had touched its malevolent cover and the pledge had been taken. I want them to swear on that rancid text that, far from wanting to sow mischief throughout history, I just wanted everyone to have a good time, all the time. I was a good human. Doing what humans do best. Trying hard to make this whole fucking swirl make sense. That my best intentions were unavoidably entwined with horror, as are all human endeavours are, is not disputed. But that is the single act of mitigation. I put it to you, the jury. No one is perfect. The defence would like to call the entire course of human evolution to the stand.

×

My friend Pat Gloom was a lute player in King John's travelling minstrel troupe. The band were called The Pageants and were the monarch's favourite beat combo. King John was a party enthusiast who insisted on checking out all the local nightspots when on military campaigns. If no spots were forthcoming he would get his courtiers to set up elaborate makeshift warehouse spaces made from military tents. He would invite local allies and those barons still friendly to his cause to join him and his knights in acts of ritual debauchery. The minstrels would then play for as long as the king and his friends were still standing. Recently he had embraced DJ culture and added acid house parties to his list of post-battle distractions. It was due to this fondness for all-night raving that John had lost all of England's possessions in France, and why the barons of his kingdom were currently keen to cut his head off. That and the fact he was constantly asking them for money for the hire of sound systems, military campaigns and the gear needed to keep him and his knights as high as balls for days. This was what the *Magna Carta* was designed to stop. At Runnymede, a bleary-eyed King John, fresh from a Sunrise orbital rave, had been compelled to sign a declaration to leave the barons' pots of gold in peace, respect the rule of law as defined by the people with the largest swords, and to pay for his own fucking drugs in future. But John had been so out of it when he signed that the very next day he'd forgotten all about Runnymede and the *Magna Carta* and was on the phone to Stabby Keith of the Naughty Boys MC for supplies, on tick, for the upcoming campaign. Stabby Keith had called up Baron Bob, marshal of the army of God and leader of the barons of England, to check if he was cool picking up the tab for 10g of nonsense and a bag of pingers. Baron Bob blew his lid, and it all kicked off. It was war and King John was on tour. Pat Gloom had called me from a phone box in Lincolnshire saying they were on the road with King John and that the whole tour had been a gas. The king's looking for DJs, he said. Knowing that I was keen to get into it, would I like to try my luck as a royal rave pilot.

This was the first dilemma. One of the many choices that the new acid house revolution would force me to make. This was not a doctrinaire movement. It wasn't a movement at all. It had no manifesto. The very act of coming together and committing to losing yourself in the ritual of dance was heresy enough. It required no pamphlets or creeds. But it did require radical freedom. You had to choose to join in. You had to choose to let the beat hypnotise you. Now I was being asked to make another, less palatable, choice. Should I look to further my disc jockey career? I had no conception of djing actually being a career, because careers are, after all, death. Or should I try and stay true to my principles and save the acid house scene from a takeover by the super-rich and their capitalist stooges? Knights and kings have no part in the idealism of drums and bass. There are no crowns in the basement. But the attraction of celebrity patrons and the chance to rub shoulders with the cream of royal society was too much for a weak-willed Jonah Plantagenet. I was an ex-existentialist from Chaffinch-On-The-Hill, a simple DJ who had sucked out the knowledge from the best players in Manchester, a faulty human from a long line of faulty humans who was keen to inflict his taste on the world. I rolled up my belongings in my travelling sack, packed a record box with as wide a variety of sounds as I could fit in it and headed off to join King John's army.

The Pageants were jamming out the last chords of an extended madrigal, and the mud-spattered knights, some still covered in the gore of battle, were jumping up and down in a frenzied collective pogo. The king was headbanging, waving an eviscerated bone torn from the carcass of a sacrificed animal above his head like a conductor's wand. It was wild. I'd only arrived in the camp a few hours before. Pat Gloom had introduced me to the master of the revels, a fidgety man who looked like he hadn't slept for days. He was rude. Everyone I met was rude. This wasn't acid house at all. The landed gentry, the king's camp followers and his courtiers were a surprisingly unsophisticated bunch. Drifts of snow-wash denim, jumpers tucked into pegs, micro-collared suit jackets with the sleeves rolled up, even a few mullets. I tried not to judge them. The acid revolution was in its infancy, and some had yet to get with its faux hippy style. I checked out the set-up: two Technics 1200s and a Tandy 'Made 2 Fade' mixer. No monitor. No cartridges for the decks either, so luckily I always brought my own. It was a shit set-up for a royal function. I'd always thought they prided themselves on their logistic efficiency. But I was near enough to the speaker to use it as a monitor, so I relaxed a little. But only a little, because

I was terrified. Though I had sucked deep from the minds of some of the realm's greatest DJs, this was my first attempt to actually entertain a crowd of people who weren't my friends. The Pageants ignited some flash bombs to indicate the end of their set. I waited until the smoke had cleared and the wild clapping of the knights had subsided. An eery silence fell in the royal rave. Bloodied knights, smashed on pillaged wine, looked about in confusion. One or two shouted for music. I'd heard it was cool to let expectation build in the room, so I took my time cueing up the first record. I had delved into my bag of tunes and was decided on a proper journey of musical education. These public-school types would love a history lesson, I thought. I had a killer reggae version of 'Why Can't We Live Together' by Tinga Stewart to kick things off. This would not only be familiar to any self-respecting raver via the Illusion or Kongas cover versions, or even the Timmy Thomas original, which were all popular in the clubs, but it would also strike a loved-up tone of reconciliation and peace for battle-weary knights. The perfect start to an epic adventure through sound. That's what I thought. I would swiftly follow this with a more up-tempo number to get things going. I chose Frankie Gee's version of 'Date with the Rain', which had been or was about to be a club smash in the hands of Jamie Principle. Connections through time. That was what I was thinking. I closed my eyes and let the vibes flow through me. Why can't we live together? Tell me why. That was the lyric.

A chicken bone sailed through the air and hit me hard on the forehead. I opened my eyes. The dancefloor was empty. Most of the knights had headed off to the bar, but some of them had remained. They were not happy with my selection. I rapidly cut in Frankie Gee. A pewter cup sailed towards the decks, knocking the needle off the record. Thankfully it wasn't the deck that was playing. I ducked down to rapidly rifle through my records looking for something these angry warriors and their camp followers would dig. I pulled out 'Action 78' by the Erotic Drum Band. Todd Terry had sampled it. It was a big, big breakbeat and so I was sure this would do the trick. I whipped the fader across as the familiar loop kicked in. A hearty battle cry rose from the crowd. I could see King John angrily pointing at maps and at me, pushing model castles around and calling for action. Knights returned from the bar with swords drawn. Ranulf De Blondeville, the most loyal of the king's nobles, was hastily building a siege tower from discarded dishes while a group of archers were poised to unleash a volley of arrows towards the DJ box. My set was not going down well.

One thing that being an ex-existentialist has taught me is that one must make choices. The facts of life are harsh, but so is the responsibility of freedom. Luckily for a compound being such as myself, choices can be more a case of hedging your bets rather than dramatic life-changing decisions. Here I was facing being hung, drawn and quartered by the King of England for my unsatisfactory record selection. I could stand my ground and die happy in the knowledge that I was a truly underground disc jockey who refused to compromise his art under even the most extreme negative crowd reactions. Or I could make a deal with the devil, my father, and not only keep the angry throng happy but also become incredibly wealthy into the bargain. I decided to do both. Reaching into my pocket for my dad's Swiss army penknife, I stabbed myself vigorously and repeatedly in the palm of my hand until it was slick with my blood. I pressed the bloodied palm to my face until it too was bright red. I began to chant as the first arrows imbedded themselves in my record box. 'Ar rut put zoom knee clak, In zim ze bang oof clue ni klop.' I splintered into bits. Not for the first time, I sent myself down different paths. I would be a worthy techno purist, a breakbeat crate digger, a northern soul aficionado, a complex minimalist, a jump-up drum and bass wizard, downbeat ruler, trance champion. But here and now I would become the world's first superstar DJ.

At this very singular point in time, I could see the enormous commercial possibilities available to an unscrupulous vampire like myself. I would suck out the essence of acid house and turn it into a saccharine product for my own ends. I would upend the rejection of rock stars in favour of collective joy that acid house had promised by making the DJ the star. In the acid house, eyes were turned to each other, arms waved from podiums over the collected mass of dancers, each dancer blessing the next. What you had? Where you from? A joining together of disparate people under the strobing lights. I would change all that. I would build stages and put the DJ at the centre. I would shift the focus from the faces and eyes of others and on to the solitary figure playing other people's music. I would turn bodies and heads in one direction: towards the DJ. They would become the rock stars. They would receive adulation. Sign autographs. Pose for photos. The music would be forgotten. The dancers would be forgotten. I would start an industry around it. Magazines. Management. Contracts. Here, now in the court of King John in the midst of the First Barons' War, I would turn idealism into profit. Idealism never pays the bills; I'd leave that to my other incarnations. They could feel good about themselves while I swanned about on my golden yacht with my celebrity friends. Fuck the underground and its hand-wringing platitudes about authenticity and keeping it real. I'd keep it unreal. I'd do what all the other DJs did, but I'd do it with confetti cannons and the most populist, crowd-pleasing, Pavlovian signature tunes I could find or pay someone else to make for me. I was going to be a star. No basements for me. It was going to be private jets and champagne from now on. The only chopper I would face would be the one laid on for my use by fawning promoters. I stuck my bloodied face up from behind the decks. Reborn as an entrepreneur. I could see Ranulf De Blondeville's siege tower approaching. I felt strangely calm as I resigned myself to a life of success and DJ excess. I casually slipped the next tune on to the turntable. I switched 'Action 78' off, letting it slow down until it was nothing more than a grinding drone. I put my fingers on the edge of the disc and began to inexpertly cut and scratch the beginning of the next record. The siege tower paused. The knights' swords froze in mid-air. Archers relaxed their bows. Pppppp. Ppppp. Wickey. Ppppppuuu. Pump up the jam. Technotronic. Once an underground sound, now number two in the hit parade. The whole dance blows up. The party continues for days in the same frenzied fashion. I'm forced to play a few numbers more than once or cut between two copies of the same record, sometimes for hours on end. I play the la da dee la da da chorus of Crystal Water's 'Gypsy Woman' for seventeen hours straight. When the party finally winds down, I'm summoned to the presence of a heroically smashed King John. He tries to focus on me, but his eyes are on different paths, so he closes them instead.

'I was bang into that set, man,' King John says. 'Proper peaking performance. I'd love you to be my new court jacking jester. What's your DJ name?'

'Jonah Plantagenet,' I reply.

'Good name! Are we related?'

A few hours later in another dimension, the more musically adventurous version of Jonah Plantagenet is in the Swinging Sporran tavern with Dizzi and God. We are rolling drunk. The tavernkeeper maintains a steady stream of honeyed mead flowing to our table as we shoot the shit out of it.

'To me, all this attention in the media is just attracting the wrong sorts to the parties and diluting our scene,' I opine in my Michiko Koshino blouson jacket.

'Nothing like a moral panic to attract the spivs and sharks,' adds Dizzi. 'I'm more interested in the psychedelic end of jazz. You know, I think I can take the freewheeling love vibe of acid house and fuse it with some out-there players, make it fresh and relevant. Tight but loose. Get the Mods into it. Get house heads into Sun Ra and the Art Ensemble of Chicago too. I was going to call it "Acid Jazz",' he continues, looking inspiringly misty eyed.

This was just the sort of fusion of new and old I could really get behind. 'That sounds like heaven, Dizzi,' I say. 'I see you've got into the rave scene,' I say to God, drunkenly waving at her Altern 8 outfit. 'Bit mainstream for me, I must say,' I add with a superior air.

'I'm really not into those big raves, if truth be told.' God purses her lips and fixes me with a steely gaze. She slowly shakes her head and lets out a sigh. The smell of strong liquor merges with the scent of her heavenly breath. 'Fucking humans. And you were doing so well, too. I don't know much about humanity, but I'm beginning to get the impression you are born elitists. A species of snobs and pretentious pseudo-intellectuals. Oh, the animals wouldn't understand, the fish wouldn't understand, the women wouldn't understand, the workers wouldn't understand, the ravers wouldn't understand. Well, you know what?' God was waving her

Altern 8 mask in my face now, her words slurring as another cup of mead headed down her throat. 'It's you who doesn't understand! You, Jonah Plantitornot. Tagignoent. Plantigeeeenit. You, whatever your fucking name is. The acid house is a big new church, without priests or popes. It's the new Reformation. The new covenant between man and machine. Cyborg and God. The rave is where it's at, man, not the guestlist queue with yer fancy mates. If you want me to spare you, y'all better get that into your heads, man. Woodstock '69 man, this is a free festival right?'

'But what if you bought a ticket?' I asked. 'Wouldn't you be pissed off if everyone just jumped over your proverbial fence?'

'Fence? Fucking fence! Fuck off, Jonah! Look, thanks for all the tips on what makes humanity worth saving and whatnot, you've made some valid observations, but this raving scene has really got me. It's a reset after the last century of shit. War and the free market. Hell, it's the best thing since the trumpets at Jericho. If we'd had the Prodigy in heaven there would never have been such a thing as the fall. Santo would have stayed, and you lot would never have been born. But seeing as you were, and the universe is stuck with you until I say otherwise, you better make the best of it. The collective is where your hope lies, take the rough, man, take a bit of rough and let it be a contrast to the beauty, because you can't keep it out. No door policy or 'No Teds' sign will keep it out. Someday they will come knocking at your door, the evil ones, the growling men, the thieves and ruffians. Stand Jonah. Stand and let the ruffians smash themselves against your raving rocks. How do you know what's in someone's heart? Is it the shoes they wear? The size of their bank balance or the cut of their cloth? How can you tell a fellow traveller if you won't share the map? Eh? Eh Jonah, tell me that! Anyway, we are all fucking Teds, Jonah. We are all ugly philistines to somebody. So, open the doors, man, open the doors and let them in.'

God finished her speech. Dizzi and I gave her a round of applause. It was a stirring, if somewhat slurred, call for unity. I smashed down a tequila slammer.

'God, I hate ravers. No class,' I slurred.

God put her head in her hands. There was no hope for any of us.

16

A brush

'A real artist may create her picture in a lonely desert ... gods look over her shoulder; she creates in their company. What does she care whether or not anybody admires her picture?'
Rudolf Steiner

Lights are dimmed in the courtroom as a dancing beam cuts across the gloom. The beam has been launched from an old-time film projector. Grainy black-and-white images are moving across a portable screen. The crowded courtroom watches the grotesque images through their fingers. Some throw up into wastepaper baskets. The evidence against the defendant grows. The prosecution paints a picture of a restless dilettante unable to find success in any given field, but with a tenacious belief that he somehow deserves to be lauded by the art establishment. Music was a dead end. Being underground was never going to pay the bills. He'd sucked all he could from it. But art. Especially modern art, with its freeform, no-holds-barred, postmodern openness. Art would be the perfect place to deceive and steal. If only he could use long enough words and wear the right hat, the general public could be fooled into finding his work profound. The film flickers on the screen. At least he never tried acting.

×

We are and will continue to be the Mods. It's the mid-1990s in the swinging heart of the United Kingdom. It's the four-teen thousandth Mod revival. The scruffy greebo grunge nihilism of the last few years has been replaced by Adidas trainers and button-down shirts. Desert boots are back. In the acid house I'm subverting the norms of electronic music by peppering 4/4 beats with electric guitars and ripped-off speeches by gurus of the counterculture. There is experi-mentation and genre blending afoot. In 1983 I had severed a lock of my lank, greasy hair and let it burn in the flames of my time machine altar. The smoke reconstituted itself in the fall out of the handbag wars. 1994. Techno trousers worn to signal a DJ's disdain for the saccharin commerciali-sation of house music had been discarded in favour of crisp, creased slacks and loafers. There is something sharp in the air. Weller is back on the radio and beads are being worn over well-tailored polo shirts with a 1960s twist. Penny collars and pop art stripes. Pop art. The time machine shudders, and I'm thrown into the maelstrom of post-war optimism. 1994 is 1964.

One aspect of my quest that perhaps I haven't explained to you clearly is the need for me to create multiple personas across time and space so that I can explore all the various avenues of human artistic endeavour more effectively. These time travelling homunculi are grown from the cells of my original body and multiply through the different plains of the multiverse. It's inadvisable for them to meet. In 1964 I'm not yet alive, but my pre-born self is doing very well on the art school scene. The world of Mod that had eluded my hippy space rock self in the 1980s is making a lot of sense now. I'm starting to dig the bold futurism of its outlook; here in the 1960s it's not retro but a zesty attempt to grasp the cosmopolitan optimism of post-austerity Britain. It's international and outward-looking. It's European, American, Jamaican, African. Attention to detail and love of sometimes ludicrous self-expression have so far eclipsed its more conservative tendencies. By the late 1960s its psychedelic love child is looking beautiful in paisley and polka dot. 1990s me sees the same great leap forward and love of the new in acid house.

'I'm still a Mod, I'll always be a Mod, they'll bury me a Mod.'
Paul Weller

I've hooked up with a bearded savant who is repurposing familiar, everyday items of consumer ephemera to create a new folk art for the twentieth century. His name is Peter Blake. Within a few years Peter and I are to become the two darlings of the British pop art scene. Poor Peter. I stole a lot of gigs off him with my time travelling thievery. I'd already stolen Rauschenberg's pallet and pre-empted Warhol by knocking up screen-prints of Mao and a promising young tyrant called Pol Pot who'd just taken control of the Kampuchea Communist Party. I did disaster tableaus in garish pinks, collages of electric food whisks and lethal injection scenes cut from magazines. It was edgy and dangerous and sold like hot cakes. In 1965, off the back of my notoriety, I designed the cover of *Help!* by the Beatles using several cut-up images of music hall stars, victims of medical malpractice, cross-country skiers, supersonic fighter test pilots and TV chefs, making it the most celebrated record sleeve in history and announcing the arrival of the counterculture. I let Peter have 'Self-portrait with Badges' and a few targets, and he did very well out of it. We were often pictured falling out of West End nightclubs with our celebrity friends. Life was good. But the streams were becoming dangerously entangled. By 1994 my DJ-based music production self was ingratiating himself with the newly resurrected Beatles and was planning their comeback album, which was to be a co-production with the Fab Four, Peshay and Roni Size. Simultaneously, my pop art homunculus was receiving praise from a new generation of Brit Pop artists eager to inject some swinging London cache to their feel-good anthems. Record launches were becoming a nightmare. If artist met remixer there would be a cataclysmic rupture in space time that would spell the end of all things. Art me was thankfully past his prime when it came to late-night engagements. DJ me was a relentless pill-shovelling cyborg. So, I thankfully passed myself moving in opposite directions through the revolving doors of life. The turn of the century was easier. The Beatles were into clean accelerationist art and fractal, computer-generated images, so Peter and I were left with retrospectives and the occasional sleeve art for heritage rock acts. DJ me was touring the world with *No Snow No Show: The Trance on Ice Experience* and working on his prototype hologram show with George Lucas's Industrial Light & Magic.

I'm sitting on a cold bench in Hagaparken, Stockholm. It's sometime in April 1907 at about 7pm. Sorry to be so vague, but I've been time travelling quite a bit recently. I've been popping up at various significant moments in art history trying to get my anchor hooked into something that I can steal and make my own. I need a new direction and some much-needed income. Art seems like the perfect profession to pillage. 64,000 years before Peter Blake, give or take a day or two, I find myself in a cave on the Iberian Peninsula. There are some figures dressed in animal skins carving and painting the walls. Early human types by the cut of their cloth. I creep carefully through the cave until I find a large bolder to hide behind. From here I can clearly see their work. It's good stuff. Punchy and magical. But won't do well at auction as few have the wall space to display an entire cave. I slice a groove into my arm, let the blood drip and I travel. Egyptian hieroglyphs, Mayan pots, Greco-Roman friezes, Persian mosaics, Qin dynasty terracotta, cartoons from the lost city of Atlantis. I steal the lot, stuffing the items into my duffle bag. I'll get a few quid for them down Slough market, but I need something I can call my own, someone's ideas I can pass off as Jonah Plantagenet originals. The ceilings of cathedrals, alive with striking religious iconography. I'd like to chip it off and make away with it, but it's too fucking high up. Stylistically it's way too detailed for my limited abilities; even if I do manage to suck all information out of the artists, it's all too fiddly for me. I need something that will express the thought and feeling of objects. Nothing too literal. Something that will capture the true sublime mystery of all things.

Every month without fail since the Tate Britain opened its doors in 1897, I have stood in front of a picture of such staggering power that even after 125 years of study I still could not penetrate its depths. 'Death on a Pale Horse' by J.M.W. Turner. Featuring a knackered death, half-pissed on the back of a ghostly steed. This is the death I know and love. Emerging from the haze after a long night in the tavern. She isn't as haughty and proud as she is often portrayed, nor is she a silent harbinger crooking their finger, beckoning you to cross the River Styx. Death is actually quite fun once you get to know her. Death isn't a bad horseman either, despite appearances. I'm guessing J.M.W. Turner caught her showing off, trick riding after a skin full. However he did it, he certainly caught the mystery of death perfectly. This was just the sort of abstraction I could aspire to. If I could get him alone I would deploy my vampire suckers and suck all the good ideas from his mind. But just when I thought I had Turner nicely isolated in a shepherd's hut and prone for a good sucking, I had second thoughts. I couldn't hope to pass his work off as my own. It was far too instinctive for a lazy vampire. I would have to unlearn skills I never had. So I jumped into the time lanes again. Into the murky hum of the twentieth century. Mass production and the machine age. How would the artist react to the mechanisation of industry or the industrialisation of death? By letting these new entities have their say. A kind of spiritual materialism. I found myself behind a technical drawing board in 1920s Dessau, Germany. Across the classroom from me I could see Herr Stuber deep in conversation with Walter Gropius. They were poring over some sketches. These were obviously plans for Herr Stuber's headquarters in Chaffinch-On-The-Hill, where the Venusian fleet would dock and unload supplies for the commandant and his family. I'd never appreciated the clean Bauhaus lines of Herr Stuber's garden shed until this moment. He acknowledged me with a curt nod before returning to his conversation with Walter Gropius. All around me my fellow students are trying to reconcile the logic of machines with the bright chaos of reality. Like Lee Perry in the Black Ark or Adonis with his 808. Wassily Kandinsky wanders in holding a freshly painted canvas.

'Hey, Wassily, that's nice, man, what is it?' I ask, leaning back on my beautifully efficient stool.

'Thanks, Jonah. I'm calling it "Circles in a Circle",' he replies, holding his work out at arm's length while studying the explosion of colour and geometry on the canvas. I look around the classroom. Everyone is busy at their desks dreaming up a better future.

'Fancy a coffee, Wassily?' I ask, staring at my blank page. 'I'm about done here.'

'That would be lovely. Have you been to the Herod's Seed Cafe? They do a very nice lemon drizzle cake.'

We descend the clean lines of the Bauhaus staircase. It's all bright, clear glass and concrete. Nowhere to discreetly enact my crime. Fucking modernism, man – so transparent. I need shadows. Wassily Kandinsky reaches the ground floor just ahead of me. He pushes through the red door that leads out into the piazza where the Red Baron, my three-speed racing bike, is chained to some railings. By the railings there is a low-lying ancillary building where the school's heating boilers are housed. Wassily leans against the door of the boiler room as I fumble for my bike lock keys. He is lost in a reverie of possibilities for his bold new vision.

'I'm looking for the hidden spiritual aspects of everyday objects, man. You know the inner beauty of the things that surround us?' he says, using his free arm to encompass the trees, grass and concrete structures of the school. He's got 'Circles in a Circle' under the other arm. I look up. Smile weakly. I pick up my bicycle lock and clout Wassily Kandinsky round the head.

'That's fascinating, Wassily,' I say whilst pushing him through the grey boiler room door and into the dusty, humid interior. Inside, it's dark and smells of oil. Kandinsky drops his painting and tries to push me away, but I'm pretty buff from all the mandatory physical jerks and group hikes we undertake in the Bauhaus school. I press on with an expressionless determination. He doesn't have much time to protest as I deploy my vampire suckers and drain the ideas, patterns, pallet and inspirations out through his wide, unbelieving eyes. He is delicious. I find all the inner beauty I can manage at one sitting. I belch. Apologies, but this one was super filling. Wassily Kandinsky is soon reduced to a thin slither of skin. I think about throwing his remains in the school's incinerator, but given time and nourishment, I reckon Kandinsky can be reinflated. No problem. So it seems wasteful to kill him. I'd like the record to show that I was merciful on this occasion; in fact, I would say that I have something of a merciful streak in me. It's a weakness of mine. Pity. God, he looks so ... so ... flat. I hope Wassily doesn't hold it against me when he's finally fully reinflated. Can the record please show a degree of reflection and maybe even a hint of remorse here. I might be a fiend, but I'm no monster. Well, that's not true either, but come on, I'm doing my best here. He'll be fine, he's still got some great paintings inside him. Plenty to live for, assuming of course he does live. I think it's a measured mugging; he's still got the whole 'Great Synthesis' period and one or two late Bauhaus works in his brainstem. I couldn't manage them all this time, not with the likelihood of discovery necessitating brevity. I've eaten my fill and it's time for me to flee. From experience he won't remember much, and anyway, I'll be off out of this time period soon enough. I pick up the canvas of 'Circles in a Circle' and hide it under my overcoat. If I hurry I can make it back to the Philadelphia Museum of Art before closing time with my new masterwork. They're bound to give me a few quid for it.

'That fucking arrogant arsehole! What does he know about art anyway? Too busy. I'm too busy. What a whining prick. Rudolf Steiner can go fuck himself, the theosophic cunt!' I'm still in Hagaparken, Stockholm. It's already dark. There is an agitated woman pacing up and down the path. She's cursing the patriarchy and, specifically, the anthroposophical firebrand Rudolf Steiner. I screw up my eyes to focus on the angry figure in the thickening darkness. I recognise the voice. Why of course it's Hilma af Klint, the

Swedish artist. Magician of form and colour. This could present an opportunity. I'd met Steiner a few times in early twentieth-century Germany. Interesting guy. But easily distracted. He'd been lecturing at the Royal Swedish Academy of Sciences, expounding his ideas on spiritual enlightenment and the creative process. Hilma was in the audience digging the message. She'd approached the ascetic-looking Austrian at the end of the lecture, hoping to persuade him to check out her paintings, but he was meeting friends at a Norwegian black metal gig that evening and wanted to get back to his hotel to apply his corpse paint, and so had politely declined the offer. Hilma was pissed off. I mean she didn't need his approval or anything, but this cat was a big cheese in spiritual theory and practice, so an endorsement would be cool. Steiner was a dick for not going. I knew her work and it was fucking unbelievable. Like the channelling of invisible forces through paint. A seance brought to life in bright, ethereal tones. Patterns and sigils, swirling lines and heavenly geometry that, like my old friend Wassily, spoke the language of the sub-atomic dimension. She was the hand that translated the voice of the hidden world. No Norwegian black metal gig would dissuade me from checking it out.

As I have stated previously, possession is not a simple case of floating into someone's consciousness and taking control of them. It requires physical interaction. But to assume someone's form is an entirely more complex procedure requiring a lot of very messy hacking. I prefer possession, personally, but on this occasion it would provoke too many awkward questions. Rudolf Steiner was a big, big fan of Norwegian black metal, particularly the work of Entrails of Babylon who were playing at Café Riche tonight. If he were to miss the show … well, it was unthinkable. Steiner would be down the front giving his best devil horn salute, and if he wasn't then the police would most likely be involved. So, I was going to have to clone him in some way. I'd not done this before but how hard could it be?

The floorboards are creaking in the Hotel Damm-Hög. They've recently modernised the fixtures and fittings, but these old hotels hold their age deep within the bones of the building. Creak. Squeak. I'm looking for room 23. Steiner always stays in room 23. This much I know. Creak. Squeak. I'm carrying my doctor's bag full of surgical tools. Clank. Creak. Squeak. It's getting late. Entrails of Babylon will be on soon. I must work fast. Here it is. Room 23. I put my ear to the door. 'Debauched Skull' from Entrails of Babylon's second album is coming out of some tinny computer speakers. Steiner's got metal on his laptop. I can hear guttural humming as Rudolf sings along to the Satanic invocation. Graaaaa. Clank. Creak. Squeak. I fiddle about with the lock for a bit, then … click. I'm in. Steiners in the bathroom. I can see him through the crack in the door. He's just adding some black rings over the corpse paint to draw attention to his eyes, which he has filled in with bright red demonic contact lenses. Graaaaa. Squeal. Chug. Boom. Entrails of Babylon are hitting their stride on the MacBook Pro 16. I almost trip over a pair of thigh-high cloven hoof boots, presumably Steiner's chosen footwear for tonight's gig. Squeak. He's coming out the bathroom. Fuck. I jump into the tiny gap between the bed and the wall, holding my medical bag to my chest like a stone knight on a tomb top clutching a broadsword. Steiner checks his reflection in the mirror. He's got a cool black velvet cloak to wear over his black leather get-up. He looks very metal. He secures the silver clasp and sits on the bed to better get into his cloven hoof boots. Grunt. Graaaaa. I jump from out of my hiding place wielding my medical bag like a mace. Clonk. Thump. What a lucky hit; Steiner's out cold.

'Ar rut put zoom knee clak, In zim ze bang oof clue ni klop.' I chant a ritual summoning spell in the ancient tongue of the fallen angels.** I use the sachets of instant coffee to create tiny sacred mounds and the sweetener to form a magic circle of protection as I continue my ritual chanting. 'Ar rut put zoom knee clak, In zim ze bang oof clue ni klop.' I reach into my medical bag and produce a bone saw. I bless the blade and hack off Steiner's left hand. Blood gushes out onto the freshly lain carpet. Fuck. Fuck. I grab a towel from the bathroom and do my best to soak up

---

** Please note: if you are the actor voicing the audiobook, an exact phonetic replication of the last sentence will result in the manifestation of demons, so remember to embellish your delivery a little.

the gore. I place the severed hand in the middle of the coffee-sweetener circle. I dip a wooden tea stirrer in the blood of the Steiner stump.

'To the east. To the west. I invoke thee.' I touch the bloodied stirrer on the instant coffee mounds. 'To the north. To the south. I invoke thee.' Again, I touch the wooden stirrer on the coffee mounds. Granules stick to it and fall off into the growing bloody pool. Steiner makes a vague groaning sound. He's coming to. Clonk. I bash him again and he's back out of it. The room suddenly fills with darting arrows of light. The walls turn to a delicate pastel shade. Patterns dance on the wallpaper like beautiful blossoms swaying in the breeze of a summer's day. It's mesmerising, just like one of Hilma's paintings. The severed hand of glory starts to dance and sway like the patterns on the wall. The hand grows taller, reaching out from the hotel sideboard as if it's climbing into the air. An arm is forming. Then a shoulder. A torso. A head. Yes! I knew it would work. Soon a near-perfect homunculus Rudolf Steiner is sat naked on the hotel sideboard covered in a thin layer of instant coffee, blood, and sweetener. He stares dumbly at me. Of course, he's not fully functioning. No worries, I can sort that on the way to Hilma's place. Steiner's groaning again. I can't clonk him this time or I'll probably kill him. Fuck his hand. What to do, what to do. I look at the dumb Steiner homunculus. 'Whatever you do, remember to keep your stump in your pocket, OK?' I say to myself. The homunculus raises an eyebrow. Scrape. Scree. Saw. I hack off the hand again and, using one of those free sewing kits you get in the better class of hotel, reattach Rudolf Steiner's left hand. Graaaaa. Side two of Entrails of Babylon's second album starts up and Steiner is stirring fast. I utter the words of discombobulation that will ensure he has no memory of these foul events, then hastily make my way out of room 23.

Hilma's studio is in Brahegatan, which is thankfully just around the corner and so I don't have an awkward taxi journey with a partially animated zombie to contend with. A quick stop in a dark alley to cut my arm and possess the homunculus with my spirit, and soon I'm ringing on Hilma af Klint's doorbell in the guise of Rudolf Steiner. She looks surprised.

'Oh, Herr Steiner, or should I call you Doctor Steiner? This is an unexpected surprise! I know you were so looking forward to the Entrails of Babylon concert, so I didn't think you had the time. But of course, please do come in.' Hilma af Klint is dressed in grey cashmere lounge wear and is holding the crust of a takeaway pizza in her hand. She was clearly not expecting visitors. I'm trying to get control of the clunky homunculus, whose facial features are gyrating around its face like a pissed accountant at the work Christmas party.

'Rudy. Please, you must call me Rudy. I'm so sorry for dropping in unannounced like this, but I simply had to come and see your pictures.'

Hilma af Klint looks confused. She had attended the lecture the real Rudolf Steiner had given only a few hours ago, and at that event the good doctor had given a most eloquent talk in a clear Austrian accent. I, in contrast, have affected the tone of a 1970s British comedy actor pretending to be a German colonel in charge of a droll rendering of *Colditz*. I sense her unease.

'Please excuse me, I have a cold,' I offer by way of an excuse. She shrugs and lets me in.

'Can I take your coat, Rudy?' Hilma asks good-naturedly, waving the pizza slice at the coat rack.

I remember the bloody stump of Steiner's hand. 'I prefer to keep it on, thank you kindly,' I answer awkwardly.

'As you wish. You've come at just the right time actually; I have some new work that I'm putting the finishing touches to that I think will interest you. I call these the trees of knowledge, and these the Swan and the Dove, and these here are some works for the astral temple.'

She waves her pizza crust at a selection of enormous canvases, so breathtaking in their scope that I struggle to control Steiner's possessed homunculus face, which kind of spins about like a Catherine wheel in glee. I'm standing in Hilma af Klint's studio, uncomfortable in my long mac, with the blood from the stump slowly seeping through the material. But the pictures have taken me out of the studio, out of my mac and the body of Rudolf Steiner, and have reconstituted me inside the dark gaps of reality. Yes, there is darkness like a medieval illustration of hell, but there is life here. There is an elegant tree with its roots digging deep into the earth. There is a monochrome swan reflecting itself, black and white like a perfect ying and yang. There are angels with gossamer wings; there are subaquatic organisms and beautiful shells. Then there is colour. Such colour! Pastel pinks blending into bold reds, while blues and yellows merge like sun and sea at dawn. Ghostly signs and the figures of blooms or spectral animals, organs, or magical symbols flow in and out of the sumptuous tones. The pictures are alive; they move and dance. This is what happens in the gaps where the human mind cannot wander. This is the mind of God made manifest. This is magic and it is real. There are circles, just like the ones I stole from Kandinsky. Circles inside circles. Heavenly intersections. They are of one mind. A magician's mind. These are images channelled directly from the astral plane. The secret life of objects revealed. I must have them. I must be them. I must steal the genius of the circles. The Dove and the Swan. I must dig up the tree of knowledge and plant it in *my* yard. Pity. There it is again. I don't think I have a conscience. Jonah Plantagenet is not cursed with that problem. I'll nick anything that's not nailed down. But here I'm faced with an impossible dilemma. Despite being on very good terms with God and somewhat reconciled to Satan, my Earthly father, I'm not yet sufficiently spiritual to pass these off as my work. I'll be found out. It's going to be bad enough when Kandinsky wakes up and is reinflated.

But these. These paintings are just too much. If I deploy my vampire suckers here, I'll most likely burst. Oh God, I'd dearly love to steal these and hypnotise Hilma into forgetting she'd ever made them. But I can't. The disruption to the timeline will be cataclysmic. No, these works are for the future to consume. This is Europe in the early teens of the twentieth century and it's about to blow itself up. In the mud and gas, in the chest-beating manly struggle between interbred royal houses, on the barbed wire and in the shit-sloshed trenches. They do not deserve these paintings. Let Steiner keep his possessed mouth shut. Men have too much to say as it is. Pity. Fuck it, I have pity. But it's a bitter pity. Let these pictures stand for a future where there is no need for pity.

A tear rolls down the undulating cheek of the possessed Steiner homunculus. Inside I struggle to contain the quivering frame.

'So, what do you think? Do you like them?' Hilma af Klint asks, chewing on the edge of the pizza crust. I manage to control the homunculus enough to muster a shrug of the shoulders.

'It's not really for me to say,' is all I *can* say.

Hilma af Klint chews on the crust with her head tilted slightly to the side. She removes the crust from her teeth and waves it towards the door. 'Righty-ho … it's like that, is it? Well, I mustn't keep you any longer. If you hurry you might catch the rest of the Entrails of Babylon gig.' Hilma pushes the confused, quivering body of the possessed Steiner homunculus towards the front door. Inside, I try to leave on an upbeat note. But I can't control the zombie's mouth, so it sounds more like the babble of an infant. Hilma opens the front door and nods her head in the direction of the dark Stockholm night. 'Fuck off, Rudy.'

17

the resurrected beatles

The court is full of acrid smoke. The jury coughs and weeps in the stinking haze. Court clerks, members of the police force and a group of sequestered prison officers are piling canvases on to a bonfire. This is the life's work of Jonah Plantagenet. His final exhibition. The judge has ruled his art to be an abomination contrary to all known standards of decency. An insult. A travesty of tone and form. A danger to the moral health of the nation. A crime against humanity. The defence has not objected and has actually been helping stoke the fires. Members of the public and representatives of the national and the international press are cheering on the destruction and have been calling for the defendant to be thrown into the flames along with his paintings. The defendant joins in with the chant. Burn the heretic. Burn the heretic.

×

I think a pause for reflection is necessary at this point. This confession has, up to this moment, been largely an account and explanation of perceived wrongdoing; however, I would like the record to show that on this occasion I actually prevented a crime from taking place. Please let the court of public opinion bear that in mind as I continue my story.

×

It's around 10.53pm on 8th December 1980. I'm wandering down 72nd Street in New York City. I've sliced a part of my body off and offered it up to the time gods in order to further my burgeoning DJ career. My blood and gore have reconstituted themselves in the early 1980s, but I'm still dressed in the outfit I had on at King John's last big post-battle rave. Doublet and lightweight hosiery, a silk shirt with a flared sleeve, Attis's Phrygian cap and some extravagantly pointy felt boots. But this is NYC, so no one seems to notice. I see a limousine pulling in up the street. Two celebrated artists are inside. They are returning from a recording studio and will soon be exiting the vehicle. I pick up the pace. Ahead is a man with side-parted black hair, slightly overweight by medieval standards, wearing a pair of metal-framed spectacles, lightly tinted. He's absorbed in a paperback book that he's reading under the lights of an apartment building's entrance. He will soon look up.

'Hey buddy, what you reading?' I ask with a friendly air. The man looks up from the book and stares at me. I see his eyes look over my shoulder at the two celebrity artists who have just exited the limousine. He becomes suddenly alert. I impose myself between him and the approaching couple. '*Catcher in the Rye*,' he answers, distractedly. He tries to manoeuvre himself around me, but I block his path.

'Hey, get out my way. I've got something I wanna give this guy.' The man tries again to get past me.

'I fucking hate *Catcher in the Rye*,' I say, kicking him hard in the balls with my medieval pointy shoe. And down he goes. A revolver drops from his pocket. I kick it into the drain as the couple pass by. It's a man and a woman. The man stops and looks down at the prone victim of my firm bollock kicking.

'Hey, man, are you OK? Is he OK? What you do to him, man?' the gentleman asks in a Liverpudlian drawl, as my victim writhes on the sidewalk clutching his privates.

'Nothing to worry about here. He just told me he thought *McCartney II* superior to *Double Fantasy*, so I kicked him in the balls. Can't have any Tom, Dick and Harry voicing those sorts of opinions outside someone's home,' I explained.

The man paused to consider the wisdom of my explanation. Then, nodding in agreement, he too kicked Mark David Chapman in the balls, before taking his wife's arm and proceeding into the Dakota Building. 'Nice get-up by the way,' he called back over his shoulder as he went up the steps. That was how I saved John Lennon's life.

The 1980s were not a happy time for the Beatles. Solo records lacked lustre and fashion choices became pedestrian. Yoko Ono produced the best work with *Walking on Thin Ice*, but the rest just retreated into twee middle-of-the-road rock. Even Lennon, spared death by my medieval shoeing of Mark David Chapman, had fallen into bloated cliché. His anti-Falklands war single 'Give Sheep a Chance' had flopped and lost him fans in the stridently Tory record industry. He got dropped by Geffen and, though Rough Trade offered him a lifeline, his album, produced by Chris & Cosey from Throbbing Gristle – in fact a tour-de-force – never saw the light of day. John Lennon was washed up as a creative force. I, of course, knew this would happen. That's why I'd travelled back in time to save him. The Beatles' estrangement only blossomed with the coming of the electronic music revolution. Again, I had counted on this occurrence. As new supergroups emerged, they began to supplant the Beatles in the world's musical consciousness. U2. Madonna. INXS. All these stadium-fillers were demonstrating a dance dimension to their repertoire. They had remixes done. They even took DJs on tour with them. I had to act to maintain the top spot in the newly created DJ hierarchy. I would surpass all my competitors by getting the biggest band in history back together again.

John Lennon is nodding out on the Funny Farm recording studio's control room couch. The studio was owned by Fish from Marillion, who bought the property with the profits from the hits 'Kayleigh' and 'Lavender' and made it into a cutting-edge recording facility. Dilly, dilly. It's my favoured spot for mixing my records. It was once found on the outskirts of Edinburgh which was nice, but it was nowhere near the kind of action I favour. So I persuaded the resurrected Beatles management to buy the place off Fish and ship it brick by brick down to Soho. It's important to get the right vibe. Location. Location. Now it's happily close to several reputable drug dealers and some top VIP night spots. I have no idea what the speakers are like or what make the mixing desk is, because I get the engineer to do all that technical stuff. I've had the Beatles out on the town all night. Club hopping. We lost Ringo at the last club; last I remember he was heading back to someone's flat with a bunch of Crasher Kids, a baby's dummy hanging out his mouth. The drums on the new Beatles album are all programmed anyway, so it's not a big problem. I'm dragging the Fab Four into the late twentieth century by hiring all the hottest remixers and producers to add their unique touch to Lennon/McCartney songs. Harrison is a worry, as his meditation practice means he's harder to control with drink and drugs. The rest I keep so out of it that they won't know what the record sounds like until it's in the shops. Pat Gloom suggests an old studio trick he uses with the lead singer of The Pageants who is forever trying to add Gregorian chants to their space madrigals. Pat just locks him in the vocal booth with a different feed from the mixing desk playing in his headphones and leaves him to noodle away to his heart's content whilst he gets on with mixing the real music. The occasional thumbs up through the glass is sufficient to keep the singer convinced he's contributing to the recording process. This is exactly what I do with George Harrison. After the recording sessions we hit the town. We go from underground to overground, starting in Crucifix Lane. Lennon, unusually loquacious despite the large amounts of Pat Gloom's quaalude and MDMA cocktail he's imbibed, is holding court in the cloakroom of Happy Jacks nightclub. This is the only spot at Sabresonic that's sonically separated from Andrew Weatherall's peerless techno hypnotism. The club contains the sound of what's happening, and I want the Beatles to absorb it. McCartney is already deep into the sound of 'Gravitational Arch of Ten' and so hasn't left the dancefloor or opened his eyes since we got here. Harrison is trying to get into the booth to ask Andrew what the records he's playing are called. He receives a polite wink, but no titles. Ringo sets up a makeshift drum kit from empty pint pots and a dustbin he's robbed from behind the bar and is making up for his lack of playing on the new record by drumming along to Djax-Up-Beats numbers. The kids are digging his style. In the meantime, Lennon is intent on getting Andrew's manager Jeff Barrett to agree on a remix for the new Beatles album. He was in the process of promising to bankroll Heavenly Records like he had the Apple boutique in the 60s, in return for a Weatherall remix. He said he'd chuck in his psychedelic roller into the bargain. Jeff was too canny to fall for this kind of absurd maneuverer. I think he sensed the hand of Jonah Plantagenet behind the project. Andrew and Jeff could always spot an opportunist like me a mile off. Integrity, a love of music and a desire to add something new and worthwhile to this troubled planet was what drove them. Even in these days of temptation, where pecuniary considerations and the morbid attraction of fame were dragging the acid dream into just another torrent of self-obsessed rapids, there was still some integrity hanging on by its fingernails. People filled with the alchemy of sound. Not the naked ambition and short-term profits I was looking for. I quite like the music, I guess, but I certainly have no integrity. I knew Lennon wasn't going to get a result here, so I hoofed up the remaining gear before anyone else could get their noses in it and suggested we check out the new super club up the road. This is where we would find more compliant artists for my schemes. The super club was great. Strict door policy, no riff raff, nice shoes, glitzy, glam, sexy, musically unchallenging but groovy enough to provide a decent accompaniment to my drug habits. King John is in the VIP with Baron Ranulf De Blondeville and the A&R department of a major record company. I love it. This is top level dance music industry stuff. The Beatles hate it. But I manage to secure a double pack's worth of premium surefire essential new tunes as the A&R guys agree on a remix package of bankable names for the new Beatles album.

The album comes out in April, a perfect primer for the festival season. It gives the kids enough time to get to know the songs so that they can sing along all summer. The Beatles are headlining every event going, from stadiums to converted supermarket car parks, and are the only band asked to headline all three nights at Glastonbury. We will visit every corner of the globe with our travelling rave-cum-psychedelic happening. It really is quite the show. The other mega bands of the age don't stand a chance. I'm the tour DJ. I'm also on a cut of the extensive merch which I helped design alongside Paul's daughter, Stella. It's been a real blast putting it together, mainly because I got the other producers I drafted in to do all the work. Executive production. I'm on points and managed to keep the rest of them on low fees and no royalties. Good for the profile, I tell them. Result. 'Rave Tripper' gets rave reviews and is instantly quadruple platinum in all territories. In truth, it's a schizophrenic mess of influences chucked together without rhyme or reason, but in interviews Lennon talks about Burroughs' cut-up technique as re-manifested in trip hop and McCartney references music hall slapstick and its connection to intelligent drum and bass. The critics are unwilling to look foolish in the face of such high concept work or out of step with the zeitgeist, so it's five stars across the board. The Fab Four are made up. Even George Harrison is happy. His mournful duet with Liz Fraser over a Herbaliser beat is one of the highlights of the album. Live, it's tricky. With no actual live drums, Ringo is given a 'Bez' role, shaking maracas and generally vibing up the crowd, while Lennon and McCartney operate laptops on a trestle table. Behind them is a vast bank of the latest keyboards and studio modules, none of which are plugged in, and a glowing Bakelite-synthesised hurdy gurdy designed by Magic Alex that has never, and will never, work. Harrison sits cross-legged on a smiley face rug thrumming a massive midi-ed up sitar. The visuals are blinding. The show culminates in a mash-up of all the Beatles favourites put together by Squarepusher and featuring live scratching by Terminator X of Public Enemy. It takes a couple of shows and liberal amounts of the special Kool Aid I help formulate for the kids to get into it, but after that everyone is totally on board with the new machine/human hybrid Beatles show. It's a plug-and-play set-up. No soundcheck required. Consequently, we have a lot of downtime on tour. I'm conscious of my conversation with God all those years ago when I was just a little boy. Highs and lows,

Jonah. Tell me about the highs and lows. Because only in the extremes will the true nature of humanity be revealed. Well, up till now, it's all been pretty high for me. I'm the most successful DJ in the world. Big paycheques. Adulation. My own range of action figures. Jonah Plantagenet souvenir Phrygian caps. High on ecstasy most of the week, on tour with the resurrected Beatles. It's all quite heavenly. So, I decide to become addicted to cocaine just to even things out a bit.

Mixtape for the End of the Century When the Sun Rises on a Bloody Battlefield

Side One

1. *Thirteenth Century Travelogue – A Winged Victory for the Sullen*
2. *Blind Architects – Dekatron*
3. *Glass – Ludwig A.F.*
4. *Trickled Away – Sven Kacirek*
5. *Orca – Jonas Munk*
6. *Alpha 2 – Ami Shavit*
7. *Ikimiz Bir Fidaniz – Kamuran Akkor*
8. *New Toytown walk – Focus Group*
9. *Spectral Ascension – Byron Westbrook*
10. *Bryce Canyon – Filter-Kaffee*
11. *Shushie Express – Sula Bassana*

12. *Western Horn – Sunn O))) and Ulver*

13. *Expo Transit System – Pocket Pavilions*

Side Two

1. *Second Movement – Bennie Maupin & Adam Rudolph*

2. *Silver Shining Bones – Dali Muru & The Polyphonic Swarm*

3. *St Nick's House – Claude Cooper*

4. *In the View of Time – Heather Leigh*

5. *Synaptic Gap – Steve Roach & Vir Unis*

6. *Good Things On the Way – Ö*

7. *Last Sunbeams of Childhood – Andrew Wasylyk*

8. *When the Light goes out, we cease to exist – Moonwood*

9. *In C – Invisible Polytechnic*

10. *The Malabaku Gang – Kobold*

11. *Velocity of Sleep - Kali Malone*

12. *Spiegel im Spiegel - Sebastian Klinger & Jurgen Kruse*

13. *My People Have Deep Roots – Arushi Jain*

18

Undoing of the Dream Drugs

Once Satan's plan had been enacted and all the little children of the Demon God had been sent out into his newly created world, Satan ran out of ideas. He had been bored when he made humanity. It was like my own Earthly father's short-lived home brewing experiment, mildly diverting but instantly discarded when the brew starting to clog up the drains. Satan lacked any form of foresight. He was reckless. He was careless. He'd made so much crap that he could never hope to keep track of its evolution. Not that he cared. He was a demon, after all. So, humanity, just like its father, tumbled into creation with little or no guidance, but still with his Satanic curiosity. That's what had got the devil thrown out of heaven. Curiosity. Just like a newborn child, he'd asked *why* too many times. But this curiosity did not extend to prolonged nurturing. The messy stuff of parenting. It was left to humanity to perfect his cruel programme on its own. I must say, we have totally surpassed all expectations in that regard. That's what I told God in one of my many reports. We are relentless in the pursuit of our own absurdity. But even in that absurdity there remains a tiny spark of the divine. A slither of the void that rests in every human heart. Dad would be proud.

×

The prosecutor looks on in bemusement as the defence council hands round a silver salver piled high with mounds of drugs to the spangled jury. 'This is most irregular, my lud. I most protest in the strongest possible terms!' the prosecutor shouts. His voice is hoarse from constant objections. The judge is fucked up beyond all recognition. He'd like to agree with the prosecutor but he's having too much of a good time. 'This is clearly a barefaced attempt to influence the jury by narcotic hypnotism,' the prosecutor continues.

The defence council pauses mid snort. 'Oh no, dear boy, my client is as guilty as sin. But there's no reason why the court shouldn't have some fun, eh. Get into the spirit of the testimony, you know,' he says, waving the rolled-up court order he's been using to vacuum up the gear at the prosecutor. 'Be my guest, dear boy.'

'Fuck it,' says the prosecutor.

The case continues.

×

It's funny how time can distort memory. It's also true that history is written by the victors. The gaps in the register of events, the recasting of roles and the denial of certain actions and unpalatable truths. History is a mess, man, but people like to try and tidy it up. It was the same with the acid house revolution. Like all revolutions it wasn't without its casualties, and like most revolutions the good stuff was quickly devoured and turned to shit. New boss same as the old boss. The human condition is exemplified by its ability to fuck things up at every opportunity. Idealism. Just another ism that needs to be discarded. I'm beginning to wonder if it ever really happened at all. The summer of love. Was it real or just another youth fad absorbed by the machine and used to sell consumer durables? The feeling was real enough. If you can trust your feelings, that is. But ecstasy can soon turn to paranoia, and love into jealousy. Who undid the dream drugs? Who broke the spell and made a mint? Who took the sponsor's coin and the TV slots? I fucking did. Jonah Plantagenet. DJ legend.

There was never really a birthday for the movement, because it was never a movement at all. But its death was one long, protracted agony. The music wasn't new, nor was its rejection of individualism, nor for that matter was ecstasy. But there was perhaps a moment when all those strands came together and captured the world's imagination. We all reached some sort of consensus, and by rejecting past societal divisions we destroyed rock stars and made the audience the focus. But I'm not sure anyone really knew what was happening; it just ... happened. The gear helped. It's hard to be Machiavellian when you're on two red-and-black caps. But myths are strong. Stories have a habit of becoming truths. So glorious was the fiction of that second summer of love that people forgot what it was really like. The media frenzy and the sheer evangelical joy of house music. This was a liberation movement. Within a few months the tiny numbers of original acolytes had swollen into a vast pan-global throng. But many people did not welcome the success of the message. 'Let's all join hands' the song said. Just make sure you wear safety gloves. The wrong sorts of people were rubbing shoulders with the elect on the dancefloor. Like furrow-browed Calvinists, the Balearic high society closed ranks. Members only. You're not coming in. Not. Tonight. Thank. You. Dress codes. Music codes. Less bleeps. Slow down. Soul II Soul loops. Nightclubs were impossible to penetrate unless you moved in the right circles. Sometimes intentions were honourable. No one wants hassle when the weekend is your only escape route, or your life is mainly spent denying who you are and the nightclub the only spot where you can feel free of judgment. No ruffians. No gropers. No fascist pigs. But at other times it was pure elitism. No one talks about that now, because now the fiction of open minds is what people want to remember. I, Jonah Plantagenet, the musical purist and avatar of the underground, was wrong. Please accept my plea of guilty to the charge of elitism fed by a desire to keep acid house for me and my mates only. DIY. Blackburn raves. Squat parties. Flesh. Tonka. Tents in forests. Generators on the backs of vans. Open doors open minds. That was the revolution. The rough becoming the smooth. Open-armed and imperfect. That was where it's at. But we couldn't see it then. But now I can. For that sin alone, lock me up and throw away the key.

But elitism and capitalism can make very happy bedfellows, as my new superstar DJ self was swiftly discovering. If we could put a rope up round the VIP tent, we could charge what we liked for entry. Humans are vain shallow creatures, so let's exploit their weakness and make a fortune. This is proper feudal system business. In the court of King John, I had turned heads away from the eyes of fellow revellers and had instead focused the attention on me, the pyrotechnic-wielding entertainer of mass consumption. Big revolutions are big business. The Bolsheviks made most of their coin selling merch to edgy late-80s clubbers. I got my head together with some of King John's loyal barons and thought of ways of maximising profits from the house music revolution. We brainstormed a few good ideas. I'd already made DJs rock stars, but now we deified them. It was essential to turn the collective experience into a finely tuned focus on individual personalities. How could we persuade the people not to merge into a greater whole, lose their own personalities and shed their worries by becoming one great entity? How instead could we persuade them to pay enormous sums of money to feel they were in the presence of a prophet whose message transcended their own petty needs and desires? How could we flog the name of Jonah Plantagenet and all the other superman disc jockeys and get them to forget about the records they played? Firstly, it was essential to talk of DJs possessing supernatural power. Give a DJ a piece of plastic and they could make it do their bidding. No longer would the records speak; it would be the DJs who now became the message. The medium was sacrosanct. Booths became pulpits. Performance overtook selection. Because, well, we were all playing the same records on the same equipment, so to stick out from the crowd you needed either a gimmick, connections, or no concept of shame. Acid house needed gravitas too. If we didn't rapidly add some serious mythology and mystery to playing records, the people might just rumble the whole project and burn us all at the stake. The barons and I came up with a plan to elevate the art of DJing into something close to a God-given gift. The bishops were called in to bless the operation. Edicts were signed and those who raised any objections were excommunicated or worse. The clergy went out amongst the people and preached to their congregations. The word spread that a divine revelation had been revealed to a new priestly cast. Tales were told by travelling bards of dazzling DJ exploits. Colossal bouts of drinking and drug-taking followed by extended sets of breathtaking variety and daring. Tales of TV themes being dropped into Italo piano breakdowns. Overtures scratched over the top of trance epics. Speeches by great world leaders sampled and plonked over generic rave pallets. House music paused as a theatrical re-enactment of the moon landing takes place under the DJ booth to the sound of 'Fanfare for the Common Man'. Famous princesses and princes pictured in flash night spots, arms around DJs. Arms around me. The bards' tales became legends. Like the *Iliad* on ketamine. With the myths came responsibilities for the hero. DJs had to embark on journeys, offer education, and if not education, then the most euphoric moment repeated again and again until the night became one great big drum roll. This was entertainment by sleight of hand. There were no downs, only one continuous up. How can you convince the crowd that they should follow this dusty old path to rock and roll cliché? Well, just like the lead guitarist of some stadium-straddling behemoth, the DJs must become personalities and pontificate about their artform. They must instil the competitive spirit of capitalism into a once theoretically egalitarian pastime. Like the swampy old rock festival there must be top billing, headliners, warm-up acts. Pay differentials. With the help of my royal patron, I granted myself the riches commensurate with my supernatural DJ abilities. Jonah Plantagenet was soon the world's most successful DJ. But others were always vying for the apex spot. Better stay on top of your game.

I blame King John. The king and those barons still loyal to his cause never really got the loved-up vibe of E. They enjoyed the rolling about aspects of the rush, the touching and the stroking. But I guess they felt exposed and, well, less special, when the collective nature of ecstasy abuse kicked in. Where LSD dissolved the self from the inside, E broke down the ego by making you want to merge with everyone and everything, outside in. It made you feel a profound connection with people and places, a realisation that the trappings of wealth or perceived social status were in fact illusory, as arbitrary as the trajectory of a leaf falling from a branch on a windy day. But when you are the country's richest man and you collectively own most of its land and the people living on it, then anything that lessens your feelings of self-importance is to be viewed with suspicion. Kings and barons are not in the habit of merging with anyone, at least voluntarily. So E was just a passing fad at the court of King John. My sets of euphoric hands-in-the-air piano canterers would only have a limited shelf life once new stimulants were available to the nobility.

Coke, of course, had been around for years, but it really became popular amongst high society after the Norman invasion of 1066. It even features in the Bayeux Tapestry, where one tableau represents two Norman knights having a nose up in a Saxon privy just prior to the Battle of Hastings. But with the popularity of electronic music growing amongst the younger nobility and, of course, with King John himself, something both stimulating but also more dignified was called for. Cocaine. In large amounts. That was the ticket. I was an early enthusiast. Initially using it to maintain the buzz of the E rush, I would scoop liberal amounts of the primo white crystalline chop the king was getting from Stabby Keith of the Naughty Boys MC into my DJ scrip and would delve into it during my extended sets. Eventually it replaced ecstasy altogether. Coke was brilliant. I was jittery but focused. Focused on myself. I found the undulating nature of piano house annoying now, and so I changed my sound. In keeping with the newfound self-absorption of King John's court, I favoured a subtle oscillation between uneventful funky garage, with the occasional vocal drop for when a fresh pile had been hoofed, and relentless mid-tempo tech house. Some of the numbers were spectacular in the right hands, but I wasn't interested in letting the records speak, I just wanted the King and his court to love me. This pattern of matching the music to the drugs became one of my greatest skills. When one of Baron Hubert De Burgh's war horses got a shard of glass in its hoof from a broken bottle of poppers, the vet, quite by accident, left a bag of horse tranquilisers behind. Baron Hubert, on one of his regular mine sweeps of the party's detritus, came across the bag and decided to have a tickle. Thus was the royal courts obsession with ketamine born. I had myself asked for a dibble dabble from the bag, and soon decided that a new brand of minimal techno would be the perfect accompaniment. Not the good kind of high concept stuff like Robert Hood, but something more palatably uneventful. I made months' worth of the stuff, and the king loved it. Then when some of the young princelings came of age and got into MDMA just like their parents, I switched to a fresh new sound I'd nicked off a deranged crusader recently returned from Vegas. I called it JRDM. An acronym for Jonah Related Dance Music. This was the sort of new musical project where all the court could really get involved. The royal architects were diverted from castle building to create elaborate stage sets on which my DJ booth could be mounted, the court alchemists conjured fire which shot from the snouts of pantomime dragons that loomed over the booth, woven from the finest silk by the royal seamstresses. Baron de Blondeville created a lever-operated riser, much like a siege engine, which would elevate me above the dancefloor during, some days, hour-long drum roll-driven breakdowns and dizzying fizzy drops. When eventually the beat kicked in, on my command, Baron

De Blondeville would cut a rope and unleash the heads of executed prisoners into the midst of the dancefloor to great applause. It was in this chameleon-like fashion that I remained at the bleeding edge of commercial dance, whilst my other self floundered about seeking that elusive holy grail. DJ credibility.

×

It's tricky to separate the defence from the prosecution. The once ordered structure of the court room has been dismantled in a flurry of reconstruction. Clerks, barristers, litigators, police and general public alike are helping reshape the forum into a pleasure palace. The judge has wired up a decent DJ set-up in his pulpit and has invited the defendant to plug in and play a few numbers. Jonah welcomes the chance to alleviate the tedium of the trial by playing some tunes to an adoring court. Jonah proceeds to wreck the joint with a blistering selection of party favourites. A carnival atmosphere takes hold of the proceedings. The judge foolishly plugs in a microphone and invites both the defence and the prosecution to make their closing arguments in the style of a crowd hyping MC. Few words rhyme with guilty and so the performance lacks flow, but the point is driven home with an admirable enthusiasm and lusty cries of *'Make some noise'.*

What exactly is the case against the accused? How can one best sum up the indictment? That he had a crack at

life and left mayhem in his wake. That he was simply following his calling. Listening to the voice of his demon.
Just obeying orders. That he wilfully stole, murdered, plagiarised, kidnapped and blasphemed. None of that is disputed. But who, hand on heart, could say they too were
not guilty of those exact same crimes? Just flicking on a
light switch in the morning causes a cascade of misery.
Power sucked from the soil. Cables carved into pristine
meadows. Populations displaced. Thousands upon thousands of microscopic lives cut short as the ugly subterra-
nean scar comes to life. How can we find a jury who is not
tainted by that same original felony? The crime of birth.
Is it possible to even get a fair trial in an age where opinions are enforced by fear of public shame and fierce trib-
alism. Where rumour and wild conjecture become facts
in minutes. Where ideology tramples on compromise and
where the political space shrinks into two armed camps
bent on each other's annihilation. Perhaps it's always been
this way, whisper and rumours becoming fact. Scandalous
pamphlets packed with half-truths and slander. Warring
factions drawn up behind barricades. The temptation to
club your opponent to death when your line of reason fails
to resonate with them. But this case offers an interesting
insight into how things might be. Because here, right now
in this dusty old courtroom, harmony has broken out as
the opposing sides swap notes, share secrets, openly dis-
cuss strategy. Defence and prosecution are united in their

opinion. The defendant is as guilty as sin and deserves everything that's coming to him. Reinstatement of the death penalty seems appropriate at this point. The solidarity of righteous vengeance. Once rival barristers are going back-to-back on the decks while Jonah screams his confession into the microphone. The jury and judge are deep into it. Everyone is lost. Lost in the sound. Legal teams cut between tracks as the crossfader shuttles across the mixer. Music speaks. Music says, 'Thanks for the lift, I'll make my own way from here.' The petty criminal is forgiven in that moment. Washed in waves of absurdity. Sentencing begins. Take him down.

✕

There is a melted copy of Led Zeppelin *II* used to shade the lamp light from our nocturnal vampire eyes. I'm in my house and the near empty bag of Seedy Sid's gear is on the CD case. Pat Gloom is checking the window constantly. Twitching the curtains. 'It's the cops,' he keeps saying. I chop out and look. It's a milk float. Twat. I've been awake for years. Everyone left the house about a week ago, but Pat Gloom said he'd hang around for a bit. Said he really wanted to hear my demos again. I'd decided to form a band and become a singer. The results were dispiriting. I felt my influence at court waning. It was all cool Britannia these days. Acid house was just a distant memory. So I'd hitched my wagon to the rock and roll machine, but that seems like a lifetime ago. I've got chop, so Pat's in for the long haul. Awards gather dust. Gold discs for long-deleted titles hang askew. The Beatles tour was ongoing, but now they favoured the angular Berlin sound. They'd moved there to be amongst it like the *Low* period Bowie. Ringo was now the resident DJ at Renate in Friedrichshain. I'm telling Pat Gloom about the wild tour of Japan in '93. He makes a magical sigil out of coke and chases it like a mouse evading a cat. I'm playing him a delicate acoustic number I've written. Just me and a guitar. Recorded live to cassette. One take. Sounds like Nick Drake. Pat Gloom lies. It's near the end of the century and I'm out of ideas. I have chop. Pat Gloom is in for the long haul.

Mixtape for the End of the Century

Side One

1. Jesus Built My Hotrod – Ministry
2. Dan, A Son of God – Swell
3. Swine – Crunt
4. No Satisfaction – Black Mountain
5. Viva del Santo! – Southern Culture on the Skids
6. 20th Century Boy – T-Rex
7. She's Got Everything – The Kinks
8. There But for the Grace of God Go I – The Gories

9. *Rumble on Mersey Square South – Wimple Winch*

10. *I Must Be Mad – The Craig*

11. *100% – Sonic Youth*

12. *Kings of Speed – Hawkwind*

13. *Sodoma y Gomorra – Grupo Geyser*

Side Two

1. *Nobody – Larry Williams & Johnny Watson with Kaleidoscope*

2. *Haunted House – Oscar and the Majestics*

3. *What Is and What Should Never Be – Led Zeppelin*

4. *Negative Creep – Nirvana*

5. *A Question of Temperature – The Balloon Farm*

6. *The Oud and the Fuzz – John Berberian*

7. *Night of the Sadist – Zuma*

8. *Psychotic Reaction – Positively 13 O'Clock*

9. *Open My Eyes – Nazz*

10. *Having a Good Time – Bulbous Creation*

11. *Play It Cool – Transfer*

12. *Space Age – The Monks*

13. *Magic Playground – Orang-Utan*

19

Death

They didn't do drummers anymore. Paradiddle rolls before the blade fell. They didn't do processions where families weep and children cry out for a parent soon to die. They didn't do jeering crowds. They did it discreetly. With levers and injections. They did it behind closed doors. There was something embarrassing about the death penalty in the twentieth century. Like driving a second-hand car or having a three-speed racing bike. No one wanted to see that. In the United Kingdom they abolished the death penalty in 1965, but much like the comeback tour of the resurrected Beatles, it was revived for one night only. For the sentencing the judge wore a specially made black cap stitched by Tommy Nutter of Saville Row. His gavel was a polished piece of rare ebony. All the court was dressed in their best designer garments. It was like the Met Ball of death. Clonk. Jonah Plantagenet: guilty as charged. The crowd in the court cheered.

Jonah's proud fist pumped the air. Prosecution and defence hugged it out. Tyburn was lit up like a stadium rock show on that night. Everyone said the prisoner looked radiant.

Camera cuts to a small boy in a massive suit that glitters with a subtle sheen in the floodlights. He looks gorgeous. A band comprised of some of the world's top players starts to perform on a stage adjacent to the scaffold. They offer the prisoner hand hearts and blow kisses from the stage. He waves and grins. Style writers file copy on new trends inspired by his execution ensemble. The crowd is of a record-breaking size. They love him and he loves them. Camera cuts to the VIP boxes. They are all there, heads of state, kings and queens, the whole cabinet and their shadows. The PM. The president. The small boy makes the rounds of the front row. Posing for pictures. High fiving. Signing autographs. The band plays a medley of his remixes and productions. The whole place in jumping. They reach the finale of their set with a rousing number by the resurrected Beatles. Then there is silence. Deathly quiet. Not even a breath is heard. The boy mounts the scaffold, and the crowd go wild.

✕

Six days. Six days of racked, rasping breathing. Six days of hand-holding and long goodbyes. Six days of family coming and going, of nurses checking in, of doctors taking readings, of bedpans and piss bottles. Six days of recounting tales of wartime exploits, of medals, of rewards for industry long since bankrupted and dissolved. Six days of remembering amusing anecdotes, nicknames for kids, nicknames for friends, stupid habits, stupid lies. Six days of tea. Six days of coffee. Biscuits. Six days of short, head-clearing walks. Six days with the sound of death screaming down the corridors. Every exhalation containing the promise of an end. The last breath. Every inhalation the body's refusal to surrender to its own ugly finale. In and out the ebbing tide of a man. Oh God, please die. Six days of guilt. Six days of wishing death on the man who had provided for you all your life. Six fucking days. The last six days after more than six years in which dementia turned a taciturn man into a helpless child. Six years or maybe more with a man changed. A gentle, helpless man. Where once there was a tough-minded business leader, now there was a sentimental old fool, his sins washed away along with his memory. Forgiven for transgressions he could no longer recall, punished by a disease that cared nothing for bombs dropped, towns liberated or profits created, for first steps, first flights, first marriages, first born. Six days of watching the body of a man brain dead for months finally run down and fade into the cold white cotton of a nursing home bed. Six fucking days. Waiting for the cycle to complete. On the seventh day, my father died.

My name is Jonah Plantagenet, and I too am dead. In as much as anyone is dead. Because if there is one thing us time travellers know, it's that nothing and no one ever truly dies – they merely change address. This is bad news for those readers who enjoy neat story arcs. For those of you following this tale who wish to see a logical conclusion, a clear and well-thought-out narrative, a good story with a beginning, a middle and an end, I apologise. Death isn't like that. It's not neat. Death isn't a bookend with your life sandwiched in between. Death is nothing. But I am dead too, so I can take the bad reviews and disappointed reader comments, it's cool. Let me tell you what happens when you die: nothing. Absolutely nothing at all. Every conversation you ever had, every mistake you made, every kiss, fuck, cough, word, song and pair of shoes you ever wore will return to nothing too. Into the gaps in between where God dwells. Nothing. Nothing is where it's at. Because nothing is everywhere. And you are everywhere, along with everything else. In nothing. So, you see, nothing ever dies because death is a no-thing, and you can't destroy a no-thing because there's nothing to destroy. Every singer you ever loved and every uncle you only ever saw at Christmas, every ant, sparrow and worm, every table, twig and atom. They are all here, now, with you in nothing. But please don't take my word for it. Please don't believe a lying, cheating, murderous vampire fiend like me. For fuck's sake, this is not a manifesto or guide to living a good life or even a good death. It's a confession.

Not long after the grotesque and yet entertaining events at Tyburn Tree depicted at the start of this chapter, copies of Jonah's confession, *Son of a Demon God,* were said to be changing hands at startling prices on the open market of heretical ideas. This was just the sort of scam he had spent his life perfecting. Convert the tedious details of your life into hard cash by spinning a yarn about your imagined cultural cache. Create a format for dissemination of said tedious details. Social media platform. Book. Scratchy recording. Rumour. Turn tedium into a tall tale. The mundane into myth. *Son of a Demon God.* Bestseller. Travel back in time and reap the benefits.

I was looking for records in a Bournemouth junk shop when my grandfather died. When I returned to the hospital with a meagre selection of scratched 7-inches, I found him serenely sleeping with my weeping mother and a strange duo of kids by his side. This was my other brother and sister, the offspring of my mother's union with Bjorn Borg's tennis coach. I have never met them before now. I can only presume that they had chosen to never leave Sweden, or that they were somehow secretly gifted proteges who had been held captive by NATO scientists and used in diabolical military projects. That or they were just secrets. Guilty secrets. The past hidden from a child to protect them. Events erased by omission. Lives never spoken of. But children are not stupid. I always knew there was a hidden anguish in my mother's life, a burden she could not bear. Now here they were reunited around the death bed of an old man. In death, all felonies are forgotten. I loved my grandfather;

he was a sweet Christian man with a little goatee beard and a criminal record. Minor white-collar stuff. Fines, no porridge. But he was a broken man too. Guilt. Lies. Hidden crimes. That's why I'm confessing all this horror to you. It feels good to get it off my chest at last. I came into the ward with my paper bag of scratched ska, bluebeat and new wave singles, and there they were, a dysfunctional unit functioning again. Mother was hugging brother and sister, and everyone was crying over grandpa, while grandpa was smiling in the void. This was the gift of death. Absolution. I had hoped to tell my grandfather about the exciting records I'd found. He liked music; hymns mainly. It brought him closer to God, like all good music does. Before I left the hospital to go on my vinyl foraging mission, my grandfather had taken my hand in his own bent arthritic hands and sang happy birthday to me. It wasn't my birthday, but it was the most perfect song he could have chosen. Because here we all were reborn, reunited and revealed to be who we really were: dishonest, faulty, beautiful humans, full of trouble and secrets. An appeal to one's humanity is not a noble thing; it's not an ideal or kernel of inner redemption waiting to be released – it's an admission of guilt. This was the first dead person I ever saw.

I was playing in an indie dance trip hop hybrid beat combo when my mother died. Once I realised musical purity was neither possible nor desirable, I had set about squashing as many genres as I could under the yoke of a sturdy breakbeat. I formed many bands with many arcane names. I had pseudonyms for the more leftfield projects and made sure my name was prominent on the more commercially viable ones. In this way I could continue to suck the life out of dance music whilst still claiming to be underground and credible. I was constantly on the road. I abused riders in every city from Tokyo to Totnes. There wasn't a band I would not add my sparkle to or a musical format that I would not add a kick drum to. This would be dance music's legacy, the subjugation of all categories of sound under the tyranny of a 4/4 time signature. Jonah Plantagenet would be the grand arbiter and pillager-in-chief. Once the resurrected Beatles had been brought under control, I travelled back through time, preventing the deaths of many other musical legends and subsequently putting them out on the road to support their new dance music directions. Robert Johnson's *Crossroads to Rave*, Otis Redding's *Try a Little Techno*, The Big Bopper, Ritchie Valens and Buddy Holly's jump-up jungle reimagining of Holly's 'Rave On'. These were just some of the projects I was either A&R, remixer or producer on. Naturally, I DJed on most if not all the tours. It was on one such tour that I got the call.

My mother had been sick for years, battling cancer with a quiet, sad fortitude. Her own parents had passed away, and I had left home for endless world tours and celebrity parties. My father wasn't much use, being from a generation that had seen their friends shot to bits by Nazi bullets and who rarely entertained emotions for fear they would be overwhelmed by the memories if they were allowed to flourish. So, my mother suffered alone in silence. But still she tried to supress her sadness with smiles. Sometimes forced onto her mouth like reluctant children on a family Christmas card, but normally her smile was the natural result of a friendly, warm disposition. She was a stoic. Never letting her discomfort show or the laughter leave her lips. But in her quiet moments, when the act slipped, in her bedroom or in the shower, when she thought no one could hear her, the sound of muted sobbing ran through the cracks and seeped into the fabric. The house on Rouge Mount Road became a melancholy receptacle of pain and loss. On my rare visits home, it felt as if the very foundations of the house were crying out for release. In those last days she could not move without help, and every subtle shift brought with it racking agony. My father would carry her to the bathroom where she would face the indignity of her protracted illness, staring at the peach-coloured tiles of their suburban tomb. Finally, it was too much. Then it was a hospital ward and morphine drips. I arrived straight from some pointless bacchanal with the stench of smoke and the residue of personal dust on my fashionable clothing. I sat by her bed, holding her hand and telling her of all my exciting musical projects as she drifted in and out of consciousness. She opened her eyes like a letterbox. She squeezed my hand with all the meagre strength at her disposal and said, 'You must be busy, sorry to drag you away.' Sorry to drag you away ... I tried to tell her that this was the only place in the universe I wanted to be, and that I would gladly trade every fucking pointless note and every turgid record I'd ever played for her just to get up from that hospital bed and say, 'Jonah, why don't you get a proper job?' But she never regained consciousness. And two hours later, still holding her hand, I watched her breathing get slower and slower, until it stopped completely. I was caught in the paralysis of hope, still believing a miracle would occur and the all-clear would be announced by amazed medical staff, but with her fingers on my mother's pulse, the nurse told me she was dead.

Mixtape for the Dead

Side One

1. Dolphins – Al Wilson

2. The Kneeling Drunkard's Plea – The Louvin Brothers

3. When Blackbirds Fly – Michael Franks

4. The Junkie Song – The Be Good Tanyas

5. Music Is Love – David Crosby

6. Your Great Journey – The Handsome Family

7. Jesus Was a Cross Maker – Judee Sill

8. Ghosts – The Jam

9. The Clown – Warm Sensation

10. *The Train Don't Stop Here No More – Don Nix*

11. *It's Raining Today – Scott Walker*

12. *Stargazer – The Zephyrs*

13. *Who Knows Where the Time Goes? – Fairport Convention*

Side Two

1. *Into the Mystic – Van Morrison*

2. *Stormy Weather – Ella Fitzgerald*

3. *Maid of Constant Sorrow – Judy Collins*

4. *Buffalo – Mountain Man*

5. *Spirit of Love – C.O.B*

6. *Wild Mountain Thyme – Marianne Faithfull*

7. *Boulder to Birmingham - Emmylou Harris*

8. *The Rain - Dando Shaft*

9. *Song to the Siren – This Mortal Coil*

10. *Deep Blue Sea – Art Lown*

11. *Never My Love – The Association*

12. *Leaving on a Jet Plane – Peter, Paul and Mary*

13. *Silent Passage – Bob Carpenter*

Look back at time … before our birth. In this way Nature holds before our eyes the mirror of our future after death. Is this so grim, so gloomy?
Lucretius

The sand drifts across the vast desert of my life. The school yard is far away in the distance over miles and miles of grit and grain. All the heads of all the victims I have sucked dry for my own fiendish ends are gone. Some have freed themselves and headed back to the school, others have dissolved and faded to nothing. All my family has gone. All my friends have gone. The Wisdom has gone. Pat Gloom has gone. Elvis Lidl has gone. Dizzi has gone too. I am alone. This is the sum of all my efforts. An endless desert of sand. Soon that too will fade and I will be left standing in the void. What a depressing ending. What a nihilistic analysis of human existence. Is that it? Is that all human life consists of: the endless acquisition of pointless accolades and pretty trinkets that will inevitably be forgotten and returned to the sand? Every attempt at improvement, every illusory step forward through the shifting dunes just another mirage? Hang on. Hang on. It's not over yet. It never is. In the distance on the crest of a sand dune, a figure emerges from the haze of heat. It begins to take shape. It's God come to say goodbye. She slides down the dunes waving. 'Jonah! Jonah! Oh, thank me I caught you before the end.' God is quite out of breath as she runs up to greet me. I wrinkle my forehead.

'The end? Why, where am I going?' I ask, slightly confused.

'Why, to your death, dear boy. You didn't think this was going to go forever, did you?' God said. 'No, no, you've done quite enough for one cycle, young man. Time for a rest, I'd say.'

'Oh. I was quite enjoying myself,' I said to God.

'Yes, yes, well, that's quite enough of that. You can't keep doing the same thing over and over again, sounds too much like a career. It's time you moved on and made way for future Plantagenets,' God said.

'But what about my mission? What about my gnostic quest to find the key to humanity's bloody existence? I thought you wanted some answers, dear God. Or have you decided to liquidate us all instead? I do hope not. I quite like it here, and I thought we might be getting somewhere at last.' I felt put out and redundant.

'Answers?' God said. 'Oh yes, well, thank you for all your hard work, but I don't need them now. There aren't any that you can rely on for too long, so it's best just to enjoy asking the questions instead. Enquiry is its own reward, Jonah. Answers don't mean shit. As for the apocalypse, that's your look out, man, but I don't think I will liquidate you, not just yet anyway. You'll probably take care of that yourselves. The universe needs contrast, Jonah. You know, dark and light, yin and yang, that's where all the tones are born, man. From silence. You see, if I was to return you all to the perfection of non-being, then that non-being would no longer be perfection – it would just be a bland drone like a beach bar mix CD. There'd be no fucking music without stuff, and though initially I was pissed off with Santo for making all these things, now I'm kind of into it. Animals and mountains are cool, man, and these threads, phew.' God ran her hand over the fabric of the chainmail suit she was wearing. 'No, I think I'll allow Santo his little indulgence this time, even if it's just to show how bad things can get. Who knows, in time you might yet turn into something beautiful. It's clear you were an unhappy mistake, with your ill-formed consciousness and inadequate limbs, but you're here now so best make the most of it. I see potential. Like in '88 when the lights went out and the kick drum slammed. Good times, Jonah, good times! But those good times are still here. It's all fucking here, man. Everything and everyone. New generations of revolutionaries making new revolutionary sounds. Sure, you'll be disappointed, that's what growing old is for. As for leaving, you ain't going nowhere, baby. Death is just a state of mind, man! You'll be around for as long as there is nothing around, and nothing is eternal, brother, so you better get into it! But remember, there's a sacrifice required. Not nice, I know, but mandatory, I'm afraid. So, you look after yourself, dear boy, and I hope the end is sweet . . .'

The last sentence faded back into the haze from which they had come as God disappeared into the shimmering desert sand. Then the sand too began to fade. My mind wandered as a new scene took shape. Sacrifice. I didn't like the sound of that. I'd already comprehensively sliced and diced myself travelling through time. I'd spilt a lot of blood, and not just my victims'. I was pretty much drained myself. Plus, I was expecting a harsh sentence from the court of public opinion once my memoirs had been published, so the thought of further sacrifice struck me as being unfair. The sand condensed into stone. The sun transformed into guttering torches. The heat of the desert turned to the chill of an autumn night. I was lying on a basalt altar. Around me the moaning incantations of millions of souls shook the air. I recognised the surroundings as the back garden of my house in Whalley Range. That pad I'd bought with the riches of rave, stolen art and plagiarised prose. The Victorian monolith where I'd sucked the minds of Mike Pickering and Jon Dasilva and experimented on captive clubbers in my basement. The crucible of creation where a great DJ career had been born. Now here I was again. Of course, the ritual. The one I mentioned at the beginning of this confession. See, story arc, dear reader. This is how the circle closes. Blood must pay with blood. Without death there can be no renewal. There was a new generation of hungry beatniks waiting to be born. Get out of the way, old man, this is the new revolution. I've occupied enough space for one lifetime. New wonders are knocking. Time to let them in. I sigh. It's been a blast but looks like time has been called at last. A shadow passes over the night sky. A demonic figure towers over me, staring down with blood red eyes. Fire flickers in the depths, its body a muscular hybrid of goat and man, rippling and shining with foul-smelling mucus and slime.

Two long, gnarled horns curl from its forehead dripping with the gore of a thousand impaled bodies.

'Hey, Dad,' I say.

'Hey, Jonah,' replies Satan.

'Sacrifice then, is it?' I ask.

'Yup, sorry about that, Jonah, but when you got to go you got to go. It won't be bad, though. Death is the one event in your life you won't be present at. You'll be in the void with God. It's nice there, Jonah, you'll like it. Truth be told, I wish I'd stayed there myself.'

'How can you do it, Santo?' I say. 'I mean, kill your own son? Can't I hang out a bit longer? I feel like I was just getting to know you.'

Satan looks touched. He pouts, and I think he wipes away a tear from his demon eye. 'Sorry, son. Time's up.' Satan reaches into his leathery pocket and produces the crumpled bag of Seedy Sid's now-diminished stash. Inside is the bright red powder. The last crumbs of gear. Crystalline. Blood red. The colour of death. The final sacrament. Satan scoops the powder up with his stinking nail, blows it in my face and whispers, 'Here, son, this will help.' I see the sacrificial scythe glinting under an autumn moon. It begins to descend.

The static hum of a cheap lamp throwing out its dull, sickly luminosity into the stillness. Sealed double glazing shielding the anaglypta wallpaper from the savagery of the outside world. I'm lying fully clothed on top of a single bed in the spare room of a house that I haven't called home for over ten years. There's a ringing in my ears. The tinnitus picked up from too many loud monitors in too many acid houses. The irritating tone is amplified by loss. My mother has just died. My father is trying to sleep next door. I can hear him crying through the stud wall. It's like all the death he has seen in his life has just revealed itself in one condensed event. His wife is dead. His love is dead. Everyone he ever knew is dead. I have momentarily stopped weeping. My body feels sore and battered. The mental is physical. Grief is a beating administered by God. Grief is selfish. My mother lives in the void with all the beautiful things where there is no pain. No chemo, no pills, no get well soon cards, no flowers, grapes or chocolates. I am a time traveller, and I am dead too. We are all dead. But in that void, we are forever present. Bound to the living. Bound to all things. In nothing. In the twisted agony of loss, I pray to God for a sign. Just one simple word of consolation. Perhaps a visitation or a message of hope delivered by a hovering moth or signified by the hoot of an owl in the distant wood. I close my eyes, now filling with tears once more, and with all my heart I try to conjure the comforting message. A single token, a solitary expression of solace for a suffering child. Then, from out of the hideous static, the voice whispers. The voice. The voice of God. I strain to hear the words. I catch the soundless sigh. Saying. Nothing.

thank you

Eternal gratitude to David Keenan for his editorial eye and unwavering inspiration. Colin and the Velocity Press for being true believers in the good word; Paul Baillie-Lane for sharp eyes and wisdom. Sofia Hedlom for goddess behaviour and listening to my endless babble. Richard Hector-Jones, Andrew O'Hagan, David Hill, Eddy Leviten and David Solomons whose friendship over many years has seeded this tale. John Robertson and Nigel Robertson, brothers in the great adventure. Russell Brown and Caroline Hayes for steadying the ship. All ravers, artists and musicians everywhere for letting sound, word and picture have a voice.